TONY THOMPSON

SHAKESPEARE

THE MOST FAMOUS MAN IN LONDON

William Shakespeare is a rising playwright in London. Plays, as we have noted, have a strange and unsettling effect on their audiences. Writers are becoming increasingly influential. It is imperative that we determine Master Shakespeare's views on religion and politics. It would also be helpful to know what he expects to gain from his writing. I'm sure he doesn't expect that his plays will still be performed in 400 years — so what does he want?

Sir Richard Topcliffe

Full name: William Shakespeare

Profession: Actor, Playwright

Birthdate: 23 April 1563

Place of Birth: Stratford, England

Father: John Shakespeare, glovemaker

Mother: Mary Arden

Education: Stratford Grammar School. Did not attend university

Religion: Protestant (?)

Marital Status: Married to Anne Hathaway

Children: Susanna, Hamnet, Judith

Notable Associates: Christopher Marlowe

TONY THOMPSON

SHAKESPEARE

THE MOST FAMOUS MAN IN LONDON

First published in 2009 by black dog books

This edition reprinted in 2013
by black dog books,
an imprint of Walker Books Australia Pty Ltd
Locked Bag 22, Newtown
NSW 2042 Australia
www.walkerbooks.com.au

National Library of Australia Cataloguing-in-Publication data:
Thompson, Tony
Shakespeare: the most famous man in London/Tony Thompson
First Edition
ISBN: 978 1 742030 70 8 (pbk)
Series: The Drum
Includes Index
Bibliography
For secondary school age
Subjects: Shakespeare, William, 1564-1616, London (England) – social life and customs – 16th century Great Britain – History – Elizabeth, 1558-1603
942.1055

black dog books would like to thank Dr Brian Wimborne, PhD., B.Sc., B.Econ. for his thorough factual check of this book.

Designed by Blue Boat Design
Printed and bound in Australia by Griffin Press

The paper in this book is FSC® certified. FSC® promotes environmentally responsible, socially beneficial and economically viable management of the world's forests.

CONTENTS

CONTENTS

CONTENTS

THIS BOOK MAY CONTAIN TRACES OF FICTION

Each chapter in this book is divided into two sections. The first section is a fictional interview with a clown who is being interrogated by a member of the secret police. Some of these stories are inspired by scenes from Shakespeare's plays and sometimes from historical events. The second part of each chapter tells the story of Shakespeare's life, based on the evidence available.

INTRODUCTION

One night, about twenty years ago, I was sitting on a bus reading a 400-year-old play, when something strange happened. I started to enjoy it.

I was in my second year of university and my life seemed to be falling apart. My marks were terrible, I was missing classes, I was in love with someone else's girlfriend and I had no money. On top of everything, my father and I were not getting along.

The 400-year-old play that I was reading had the uninspiring title of *Henry IV, Part 1*, and it was by William Shakespeare. It was on the reading list for one of the courses I was failing, Renaissance Literature.

The play turned out to be more about Henry IV's son, Prince Hal, than about the King himself. Hal was a bad boy. He was hanging around pubs, spending all of his money and neglecting his duties. His father was furious with him and — hang on! This was starting to sound familiar. In a flash, I recognised something new in Shakespeare. His characters might be kings and princes who spoke oddly, but most of all they were people just like me. That day on the bus I became Hal, and for some reason things didn't seem so bad.

Too often Shakespeare is given to us like medicine. He is a 'genius' and reading his plays will make you a better person. Some people insist that Shakespeare is an essential part of the education of any civilised person. I always wonder which plays they have been watching.

The Shakespeare that I love makes me find the diabolical Richard III more interesting than any of the other characters. I cheer for the serial killer Macbeth and I delight in the monstrous practical joke played on Malvolio in *Twelfth Night*. The two teenagers who defy their parents in *Romeo and Juliet* get my vote, as does Hamlet, every mother's nightmare.

Shakespeare is a genius for the same reason that Stan Lee, the guy who created the *Spiderman* comics, is a genius. We love watching Lee's superhero climb walls and fight with villains, but his real appeal is that he makes mistakes, just like us. Shakespeare's characters are funny and larger than life, but he never lets them get too far away from real people. Not many of us know what it's like to be a king like Shakespeare's *Lear*. But we all know what it's like to do something really silly and have to live with the consequences. *King Lear* isn't just about kings; it's also about doing silly things. That's what keeps me coming back to Shakespeare.

I had fun writing the fictional parts of this book, because I could put away the history books and just make up stories about my favourite writer. Like all biographers of Shakespeare, I had to deal with some large gaps in the records. All books on Shakespeare's life are, to some extent, fiction. There are simply not enough facts to fill a book, so a writer must decide what happened in between and try to make a case for their story. History is a bit like that. The past is never simple.

Shakespeare's plays are good for you, but not because they represent high culture or high ideals. His plays are thrilling because they remind us what odd creatures we are, and how entertaining life can be if you give it a chance. Twenty years ago I got on a bus with a Shakespeare play. I am still waiting for my stop ...

CHAPTER ONE

THE CONY-CATCHER

Investigator:
Sir Richard Topcliffe
Subject:
Thomas Skelton

We have been interviewing Thomas Skelton, a curious individual also known as 'Tom Fool', who is supposedly set to become the next court jester. Skelton seems to be more of a petty criminal than a performer. In the course of the conversation, a name came up that we have begun to hear more and more in these interviews with theatre people. It would seem that Will Shakespeare assisted Skelton in some cony-catching and cozening of the first order.

Topcliffe: You say that Shakespeare played a joke on the playwright Robert Greene, and that you assisted him?

Skelton: Yes, you see, when Will first came to London he was acting with the Queen's Men theatre company, but they weren't paying much. He and I used to spend a bit of time with Bob Greene and some of Bob's less reputable friends at a pub in Bishopsgate. Bob was always talking. He had great plans for robberies and cons but little ever actually happened. I think he liked the idea of crime but had little stomach for the act itself.

But one afternoon, Cutting Ball, whose sister Emma lived with Bob Greene, came into the pub with the news that a group of pilgrims were arriving at Gadshill that very night. His plan was to rob them. As far as he knew they had no official escorts or guards and would be easy prey. Bob was particularly interested in the notion that they were unarmed. Will Shakespeare noted that Bob was all ready for a robbery, but only if there was no chance that he would face danger himself. While Bob and Cutting Ball made their plans, Will took me aside.

'I have a plan too,' said Will. 'When Bob has robbed the pilgrims, we shall rob Bob and perhaps cure him forever of the idea that he is a master thief.'

'And Cutting Ball? I should not like to rob him,' I said.

'I shall speak to Master Ball,' said Will. 'I suspect he enjoys a good joke as much as the next man.'

That night we followed Cutting Ball and Bob Greene to Gadshill where they stood at the side of the road and waited for the pilgrims. We were there for a half hour or so, when ten or eleven riders on horses appeared, trotting slowly up the road. Cutting Ball jumped out in front of them.

'Off the horses! All of you!'

'We are humble pilgrims, Sir, you do us wrong to—'

'Get off the horses or I start with this lad!' yelled Cutting Ball, pulling a boy off his horse and holding a sword to his throat.

I could see Bob Greene sweating and shuffling nervously. His hands were shaking so badly he could barely hold his sword. Cutting Ball told the pilgrims to empty all of their possessions onto the ground and they obeyed.

'Watch them carefully, Bob,' said Cutting Ball. 'Don't let 'em move.'

'No one mmmmove, alright?' stammered Bob.

'That'll terrify them,' said Cutting Ball dryly. 'Go easy, Bob, they're only pilgrims.'

Even some of the pilgrims laughed. Will Shakespeare was snorting quietly beside me.

When Cutting Ball had loaded all of the valuables into a large sack, he tied up the pilgrims. Bob was no help at all so Cutting Ball told him to take the sack and begin heading back to London. As Bob struggled to get the sack over his shoulder, he looked sadly back at the pilgrims and started to walk. We followed him for a while until we were well away from Gadshill. Will handed me a mask and put one on his own face. We drew our swords and rushed up behind Bob.

'Good sar!' shouted Will in a mad Irish accent. 'We'd ask you to put down dat sack. Thanks.'

Bob reeled around at the sight of two men in masks standing with swords drawn on the dark road. He dropped the sack and ran. We watched him until he was out of sight. A few minutes later, Cutting Ball appeared.

'Thanks, fellas,' he said. 'You've saved me the trouble of cutting Greene's foolish throat for his share.'

We handed over the sack to the thief and made our way back to Bishopsgate. We walked into the pub and found Bob standing with sword drawn.

'There were two of them!' he shouted. 'And I drew my sword—'

'Only two?' said Will. 'Surely you would have handled but two?'

'Four perhaps — it was dark — but I drew my sword and I said, "Do you know who I am?"'

'Only four to rob Mr Robert Greene?' said Will.

'You are right, it was nearer to seven.'

'Or perhaps nine?' said Will.

'Easily, but I took a few down with my sword…'

'These lies are a bit like the man who tells them,' said Will.

'I beg your pardon, Sir?' said Bob.

The pub crowd fell silent and everyone looked at Will.

'These lies are fat and cowardly. 'Will put on his mask. 'Put down dat sack,' said Will with his Irish accent.

Bob turned red with rage and ran at Will, who darted around the room laughing. The story got around the pub and there was much mirth at Bob's expense. When we told Bob what Cutting Ball had said there was relief on his face, and Will insisted that Bob buy tankards for both of us on account of us saving his life. He did so, but I wouldn't say he was happy about it.

Topcliffe: This Will Shakespeare is a clever fellow, is he not?

Skelton: Very clever, Sir.

Topcliffe: Too clever for his own good perhaps.

The interview moved on to other topics but we have included this transcript in Will Shakespeare's file. He is clearly a man to watch.

ELIZABETHAN LONDON, OR WHY SHAKESPEARE'S PLAYS ARE SO VIOLENT

In one of Shakespeare's early plays, *Titus Andronicus,* a woman has her tongue cut out and her hands chopped off. Later in the play, her father is tricked into chopping off one of his own hands. The play finishes with another woman sitting down to eat a pie made from the bodies of her two sons.

Romeo and Juliet finishes with a double suicide, completing a play filled with street fights, stabbings and gang violence.

Macbeth finishes with the main character's head being swung around in victory.

Hamlet ends in a massacre that kills nearly every main character.

Most of Shakespeare's plays, even the comedies, contain an element of violence. Was Shakespeare a bloodthirsty maniac? Or was he a shrewd businessman who knew what brought in the crowds? Certainly, in his time as in ours, violence and sex were what people wanted to see. Even so, it is difficult to imagine people having the stomach for the level of violence described above; unless of course, those people lived in a society where violence was part of everyday life. Shakespeare's London is renowned for its cultural life, but there was another side to the city and Shakespeare didn't shy away from it.

Shakespeare left his hometown of Stratford some time between 1585, when he attended the christening of his twins, and 1592, when a rival playwright criticised him in a famous pamphlet. The period in between is sometimes referred to as Shakespeare's 'lost years', and there are numerous theories about what he was up to in this time. In all likelihood, he got fed up with making gloves in his father's workshop and joined one of the many theatre companies that passed through Stratford. By the time he reached London he would have been taking minor roles as an actor, perhaps helping to adapt stories and older plays for performance. Will did not grow up in London, so the impression that the city made on him when he arrived would have left an enduring mark on his imagination.

The Lost Years

In 1585, William Shakespeare signed the baptism certificate for his twin children, Judith and Hamnet. He was twenty-one years old, and had been married to his wife, Anne, for three years. For the next seven years there is no evidence at all as to what he was doing. When he appears again in 1592, it is as a rising playwright in London. This period in Shakespeare's life is known as the 'lost years' and it has produced more speculation than just about anything else in Shakespeare's story.

There has been much debate about Shakespeare and the Catholic religion. Some historians who believe that Shakespeare was a secret Catholic might put him among other secret Catholics during this period. Other historians might decide that Shakespeare was a teacher, and have him pressing Latin onto his young charges throughout the late 1580s. Or perhaps, as has been put forward many times, he was a soldier and visited places like Verona, Copenhagen and Venice. Shakespeare's plays reveal all kinds of obscure knowledge on a wide variety of subjects from astronomy to botany to music. There is always something in the plays that can be used to support a claim about these 'lost years'. The witty gravedigger in *Hamlet* might be based on Shakespeare's own experiences in this profession. He may have been a gatekeeper like the fellow who answers the endless knocking in *Macbeth*. Perhaps, he was a money-lender like Shylock in *The Merchant of Venice*. The most famous story is that he was caught poaching deer and driven out of Stratford. This myth began not long after he died but is not well supported by any surviving evidence.

Sometimes it is easier to simply draw a line from point A to B and then determine the straightest path. How does a person become a playwright? They get involved with the theatre. How do they become involved with the theatre? They start as a stagehand or helper or as an actor of bit parts. There is plenty of evidence that Shakespeare acted in plays during the 1590s. It would make sense that he began as an actor and slowly developed his skills as a playwright. There are numerous references to acting and actors in his plays. In *Hamlet,* the title character gives detailed instructions on acting to a group of players. Now this may seem like the same trap as deciding that he was a gravedigger, but the line between actor and playwright is straighter than most of the other possibilities.

The 'lost years' will continue to tantalise historians and biographers forever unless a diary or a lost bundle of letters turns up to solve the mystery.

In Shakespeare's time, much of the population of London was drunk. Drinking beer was relatively safe in a city where drinking the polluted water could be suicide. The main source of drinking water, the River Thames, was filled with dead animals, human waste and garbage. So children, adults and old people drank beer. They drank it morning, noon and night. There is no shortage of drunks in Shakespeare's plays either. Falstaff, the Gatekeeper in *Macbeth* and Sir Toby Belch in *Twelfth Night* are just some of the comical figures associated with alcohol in his work. Not surprisingly, Londoners in Shakespeare's time were also great singers who sang the popular songs of the day as they went about their business. Most of Shakespeare's plays feature songs, which would have been quite significant to the original audiences. If they liked the song, they would buy the lyrics and learn them. There was no recorded music in this period, so if you liked a song, you sang it.

But drinking didn't just produce jolly singers. In a city of 150 000, where beer was being drunk in large amounts, street brawls were common. Arguments could quickly get out of hand, for as well as being very drunk, Londoners in Shakespeare's time were also very well armed. The city had a vast criminal class and there was no real police force. Citizens had to take responsibility for their own protection. Most carried a rapier, along with a dagger and possibly another concealed knife.

A fight that started between two people often drew in others, and sometimes developed into a riot. By some estimates, there were more than thirty major riots in London between 1580 and 1600 — more than one a year. There is a flavour of this in *Romeo and Juliet*. The opening scene sees a humorous exchange of insults flare up into a battle between two families. The Prince breaks it up, noting that three brawls 'have thrice disturbed the quiet of our streets'. Soon after, Romeo wearily asks his cousin, Benvolio, 'What fray was here? Oh tell me not for I have heard it all.' Shakespeare's original audience might have sympathised.

Shakespeare may have also felt he had to compete with the other main form of entertainment at the time. Bear baiting was hugely popular, and Shakespeare must have noted the high level of cruelty and violence in this terrifying 'sport'. A bear was tied to a post and attacked by dogs. The bear either killed the dogs or was killed by them. Generally the bear would win, but not without sustaining horrible injuries. Sometimes the bear was blinded to even the odds. On at least one occasion a blinded bear broke loose, causing pandemonium among the spectators.

Some of the bears became celebrities. A bear named Harry Hunks is regularly mentioned by Elizabethan writers, and another, Sackerson, is referred to by Shakespeare in *The Merry Wives of Windsor*.

In *King Lear*, a character named Gloucester is being held by Lear's two evil daughters. He says, 'I am tied to th' stake, and I must stand the course.' Soon after this reference to bear baiting, Gloucester is blinded in a moment of incredible cruelty. Clearly, Shakespeare had bear baiting in mind for this scene. The other famous reference is a stage direction in *The Winter's Tale*. 'Exit, pursued by bear' is how a character called Antigonus leaves the stage. Presumably, the 'bear' would have been an actor dressed in a costume rather than Sackerson or Harry Hunks themselves. Shakespeare wasn't going to risk being upstaged by a rival celebrity!

King Lear also makes reference to another popular sport of the time. Early in the play, Lear himself says, 'Nor tripped neither, you base football player.' There is another mention of football in a play called *A Comedy of Errors*. What kind of football was played in Shakespeare's time? The most common version, sometimes called Gameball or Mob Football, was played on Sundays. The goals were kilometres apart in different parts of the city and the objective was to keep possession of the ball. There was a myth that Gameball had once been played with the heads of traitors, but the ball was typically made of rough leather or a pig's bladder. The teams were enormous and there was no rougher sport in Elizabethan England, (unless, of course, you were a bear). As the ball moved around the streets, fights broke out, old scores were settled and shops were looted. Spectators pelted the players with rotten vegetables. One writer of the time observed that the game, 'was more a kind of fight than play or recreation, a bloody and murdering practice than a fellowly sport or pastime'. He was probably right. This kind of football is still played once a year in a town called Ashbourne in Derbyshire, England. It remains a very rough game.

When the residents of Shakespeare's London weren't engaging in drunken brawls, watching bears battle with dogs or footballers breaking bones, they were probably watching a public execution.

The worst crime that a person could commit was treason. To speak or plot against the Queen was the surest path to a slow, horrible and very public death. A treasonous citizen could look forward to being dragged through the streets to an execution site. There, several possible punishments awaited. The prisoner might be hanged, dropped slowly so that he eventually suffocated. The executioner, as a bonus, might cut out the prisoner's heart and show it to the crowd. The other possibility was being drawn and quartered while still alive, and having one's body parts thrown into the fire. The prisoner's head would then be stuck on a gate to feed the large black ravens of London, providing a vivid warning to anyone else pondering treason. On a daily basis, Londoners would see their fellow citizens being whipped, beaten or placed in the stocks for a variety of offences. Sometimes prisoners were chained to a wall below the waterline in the filthy River Thames so that when the tide came in they were nearly drowned.

Cony-Catchers, Cozening and the London Underworld

'Cony-catching' and 'cozening' were Elizabethan terms for tricking someone in order to rob them. People were 'gulled' or 'cozened' by elaborate schemes devised by criminals. Many of Shakespeare's plays involved plots or subplots where people are fooled by others. *Othello, Much Ado About Nothing* and *Twelfth Night,* along with others, feature a character or characters who are comprehensively deceived. The vast criminal network that existed in Shakespeare's London inspired its own literature. Shakespeare's sometime nemesis, Robert Greene, wrote several pamphlets on the subject. The appetite for stories of criminals like the notorious Cutting Ball was large, and Shakespeare found ways to incorporate them into his plays. *Henry IV* is a historical play about an English king, but some of the secondary characters, such as Falstaff and his criminal gang, are far more interesting.

It would have been almost impossible for a Londoner to avoid the rougher elements of life in their city. Shakespeare sought to catch the interest of playgoers by offering them great stories and interesting characters speaking witty or thought-provoking dialogue. But he also tried to show them something of themselves and the world they lived in. So in a city like London he could hardly ignore violence.

Elizabethan London

London grew and flourished during this period. The population rose above 200 000 as immigrants from war-torn Europe flooded in. New neighbourhoods began to develop and sprawl outwards from the city, but most of the population lived within the city walls. The incredible density of people in such a small area meant that disease spread quickly. It was in this period that London became an increasingly important centre for trade, which made for a busy city but also one where the gap between rich and poor grew. The first maps of London were drawn in this period.

Queen Elizabeth

Shakespeare is often associated with 'Elizabethan' England. Elizabeth Tudor became Queen of England in 1558 upon the death of her older half-sister, Queen Mary, also known as 'Bloody Mary'. Elizabeth was the daughter of Henry VIII and his second wife, Anne Boleyn. Her reign lasted more than forty years. Elizabeth enjoyed the arts and saw many of Shakespeare's plays performed at Whitehall Palace.

Sir Richard Topcliffe

A figure of fear in Elizabethan England, Sir Richard Topcliffe was the Queen's Interrogator. He built a torture chamber in his house where he carried out terrifying interviews. His success at extracting confessions made him popular with the Queen's advisers. This dangerous man lived a long life and died comfortably in his bed in 1604.

CHAPTER TWO

VIOLENT DELIGHTS

Investigator:
Sir Richard Topcliffe
Subject:
Richard Tarleton

15 May 1587: The prisoner Richard Tarleton is a clown and considers himself something of a jester to the Queen. At a recent performance at the Queen's court he impersonated and ridiculed Robert Dudley, the Earl of Leicester. The Earl was not pleased and had the clown charged with slander. We have questioned Tarleton on a number of individuals involved in the theatre. The following is an abridged transcript of his response when asked if he knew William Shakespeare. Master Shakespeare has become increasingly popular as a comic actor since his arrival in London sometime last year.

Topcliffe: Tell us about the actor William Shakespeare.

Tarleton: Will Shakespeare? He's a cheeky rogue. He should be in here, not me. It was Will who put me up to it. I'm just a fool, a clown, the Queen's jester mind you, but just a clown. Shakespeare is a whole other bundle of sticks, let me tell you. He is a wild boy, even wilder than that Marlowe fellow — oh ya we'll get to him later — but let me tell you about Shakespeare when I first knew him.

Two years ago we *[the prisoner is referring to the Queen's Men, a theatre company that occasionally tours the countryside]* were performing in the middle of nowhere, Stratford, some dreadful little town full of nobodies making out to be something more than they are. Anyhow, I'm up on the stage making everyone laugh before the main play — that's my job and there is no better at it — and there's this boy laughing himself silly in front of me. I say:

'You're full of mirth, Sir.'

'Better to be full of something like mirth, Sir!' the cheeky lad hollers.

And the rest of these country bumpkins think this is hilarious. I say:

'You're a cheeky fellow!'

And he says:

'Oh no, Sir, you have much greater cheeks than I.'

Well, this has everyone rolling around in the muddy field and I'm starting to get a bit angry because this lad is getting the laughs. I say:

'You are a little monkey.'

And that gets a few giggles until he says:

'Well then, if I am a little ape, you should bear me on your shoulders!'

And then he stands up and imitates my walk. Now I have never been ashamed to be a hunchback, used it as part of my routine often in fact, but this made me furious because the whole audience was laughing and hopping around like apes. From the corner of my eye I could see the other actors in the company laughing at the side of the little stage. I'd had enough. If he could defeat me in wit, I wondered how his fencing skills were. *[The prisoner is, despite his hunchbacked appearance, a talented fencer. So he says.]*

'Come up here, rogue!' I shout, holding out a rapier.

He looks up at me, surprised. I think he was trying to figure out if it was another joke.

'Where's your tongue now, boy?' I bellow. 'Surely an old ape is no match for a young lad at the swords!'

He climbs up onto the stage and accepts the rapier. I knew that I had him now. This boy was obviously frightened and I decided that I would make a great show of it, knocking his sword out of his hand, pinning him to the stage and then letting him go. I meant to teach him a lesson, right. We stood ready to fight when I noticed that he was inching his right shoulder up and dropping his other arm. The audience who had been quiet began to chuckle. He then lets out a great yell and begins hopping around the stage like an ape. I decided at that moment to kill him, and began to chase him. The audience roared with laughter as he jumped away from my cuts and sweeps. He was hooting and grunting and climbing all over the set. When I started to lose my breath, I threw my sword down and stomped away off the stage. The audience booed and whistled but began to cheer again as the astonishing rogue bowed and waved to them.

The other actors tried to calm me down but I'd had enough. I went back to the inn and sat alone in my room while the company performed the main play without me. I was still fuming about the cheeky country lad. The next night in Stratford, one of our actors was caught in a long kiss with a local woman and promptly executed by her husband. This actor, Rollins I think his name was, only played bit roles but they were often comic parts and quite difficult. Well, Sirs, you can guess what our manager did. He hired the cheeky rogue on the spot. It was only later that we found out that he had a wife and kiddies and had been in trouble with the local authorities. I mean, I wasn't surprised because he was a wild boy.

You've asked me if he ever uttered a word against our Queen Elizabeth. Well, not exactly, but it's all his fault that I am in here. This is how it went:

I was ordered to perform at a banquet for the Queen. Now, you fellows know that the Queen has always had a place in her heart for old Tarleton and I wanted to make sure that I would stay in her graces forever with my wit. But, since that day in Stratford I felt as though I had lost some of my humour, and I wondered whether I should still be able to make the Queen laugh so hard as I once did. I decided, the greater fool I, to ask Will Shakespeare, the cheeky rogue, what he thought would make the Queen laugh. He said, and I'm telling you the truth:

'Robert Dudley, The Earl of Leicester, is a comical fellow is he not, with his big belly and great love of women and wine.'

I nodded but said that the Earl was one of the Queen's favourites. Will said that this had changed, and that the Queen would now like nothing better than to laugh at the old Earl of Leicester. Together, Shakespeare and I worked up a character called 'Bob Deadly', who would stumble around drunkenly telling everyone how much the Queen loved him with great winks and smirks. Will said the Queen calls the Earl's wife the 'she-wolf', so every so often I would let out a howl and say, 'Yes dear I'm coming!'

Yes, it's funny, even you are laughing… well, smiling.

I don't have to tell you fellows that the Queen did not enjoy the routine as much as I thought she might. I did spot a smirk on her face but she was trying her best to look horrified. When young Devereaux challenged me to a duel, I looked to the Queen for deliverance but she was leaving. I didn't know that Devereaux was Lady Leicester's beloved son. So you see, it was all Will Shakespeare's fault, that rogue, and it should be him and not me in prison!

The prisoner did not know anything about Will Shakespeare's religious or political views. Luckily for the prisoner, the Earl of Leicester died a week after the performance. Tarleton was released with a warning. It is unlikely that he will be asked to perform for the Queen again.

WHY SHAKESPEARE COULDN'T SPELL HIS NAME OR FIND BOHEMIA ON A MAP

There were no bad spellers in Shakespeare's time — everyone simply devised his or her own way of spelling things. Reading in those days involved a certain amount of guesswork. The man known variously as *Shagsbere, Shaxpere, Shaksberd, Shaksper*, or *Jaquespierre* used a range of versions of his own name. One that he never used was '*Shakespeare*', which became the standard spelling in the twentieth century. It raises the question of what students did at school in Shakespeare's time. They certainly weren't doing spelling tests!

Shakespeare's most famous reference to education is from his famous 'Seven Ages of Man' speech in *As You Like It*. It involves a 'whining schoolboy' heading to school 'unwillingly'. Children then, as today, had mixed feelings about school, but surely Shakespeare, beloved of teachers all over the world, must have adored school? Is it possible that the greatest writer in English was a 'reluctant' student?

In *Love's Labour's Lost* a pompous scholar named Holofernes says, 'You find not the apostrophas, and so miss the accent.' It isn't difficult to hear a teacher's voice in this character. Shakespeare made fun of lawyers and police officers. Teachers were not spared. In *The Merry Wives of Windsor,* a Latin lesson is used as an occasion for a long string of rude jokes.

When he was four, Shakespeare would have started at the Petty School. The word 'petty' comes from the French word 'petit', which means 'little'. These schools were often run by an educated woman at her house. The children would learn to read and write (though not to spell) in English. They didn't have a desk but instead sat on a small stool and learned to write holding parchment on a piece of flat wood. Students had to make their own pens. They also learned manners and useful things like how to chew food and properly use cutlery. Children were not regarded the same way they are today. The idea of 'childhood' as we know it only began in the early 1800s. Children in Shakespeare's time were regarded as little adults and expected to behave as such. Students at the Petty School memorised long passages of commentary on good behaviour and religion. The religious instruction taught them how to pray and how to behave in church.

When Shakespeare turned seven, he said goodbye to at least half of the children in his class at the Petty

School. The girls stayed at home with their mothers to learn to cook and sew while the boys went off to the 'grammar' school where they learnt, well, mostly grammar. However, it wasn't English grammar that they were learning, as the haphazard punctuation of surviving manuscripts shows us. Instead, they were learning the classical languages of Latin and Greek. The common and somewhat snobby sneer that Shakespeare had, 'small Latin and less Greek,' is based on the fact that he did not go to university. The truth is that his education meant that he was proficient in both languages.

The young Shakespeare would have been awake at 5.00 a.m. for prayers and breakfast, to be in the classroom by 6.00 a.m. A lot of time at school was spent memorising passages from classical literature. Shakespeare's plays are vast grab-bags of references to Greek and Roman stories. It is likely that most of these stories were stored in his brain. To work on their Latin, the boys debated. Every day, a grammar school student would be expected to defend a proposition, usually something historical. In Shakespeare's time, examples from English history were introduced into the curriculum, so he may have first considered characters like Henry IV and Richard III while arguing about them in Latin at the front of a classroom. This may have been the most interesting part of the day for the students, watching their peers trying to better each other in debate. Many of Shakespeare's plays involve spirited exchanges. Hamlet spends most of his play demolishing everyone in his path with his quick tongue, until he meets a gravedigger who betters him.

Playgoers have spent 400 years wondering why, in *A Winter's Tale,* Shakespeare sets some of the action on the sea coast of Bohemia when the country, part of the modern Czech Republic, is completely surrounded by land. The answer is that geography wasn't taught at school. Neither was maths. Physical education was unheard of and science was still associated with magic so was not considered appropriate for students. They learned Latin and Greek and not much else.

The teachers weren't gentle. A boy might be asked to recite a passage, say from Homer's *Iliad,* and was whacked with a stick if he got it wrong. There were no discipline problems. Any deviation from the rules was met with swift justice. The classrooms were cold and most students kept warm with a candle that they would bring from home. It was a long day, almost twelve hours of memorising, writing, debating and reciting. In the winter, it would be dark when the young Shakespeare made his way home. It is easy to imagine the seven-year-old future playwright having trouble keeping his eyes open at dinner while his father and mother discussed the day's events.

Shakespeare's mother, Mary, would have been interested in what her son was learning because she could read and write. Her signature suggested that she had learned to write and she served as an executor for her father's will, which means that she could also read. A line in *Titus Andronicus* might be another clue that she had been educated. When one character is asked about a book, he answers: 'My mother gave it to me.' In a period when less than ten per cent of English women could read, it is an intriguing reply. Perhaps Mary read to the young Shakespeare and encouraged his love of stories. Her family name, Arden, was an ancient name in the area with distant links to the nobility. Mary's family was relatively wealthy and she would have enjoyed a comfortable childhood. She inherited land from her father a few years before she married Shakespeare's father, John. Shakespeare later used the name Arden for the mysterious forest in *As You Like It*.

Shakespeare's father may provide one of the most important clues as to Shakespeare's motivation and personality. Elizabethan England had a rigid social structure, which made it difficult for most people to improve their position in life. John Shakespeare started in the somewhat lowly position of an apprentice glovemaker and leather worker. From 1556, he began to seek elected positions within Stratford. His first role was as 'Ale Taster,' which sounds like he got to drink a lot of beer, but had more to do with making sure shopkeepers were not overcharging their customers for food and drink. This led to him being elected Constable, a kind of police officer. Shortly after William Shakespeare was born, John was elected High Bailiff, a role similar to Mayor. It made him a respected citizen of the town and ensured that his sons could attend the local grammar school. It also meant that he was in charge of booking theatre groups to play to the townspeople. The young Shakespeare would have seen all the performances that took place in Stratford. Something that is not known about William Shakespeare is how he became involved in the theatre. Perhaps it was his father's role that allowed him to make some contacts with members of the London theatrical community. Hamlet's excitement when told about the travelling players' arrival might provide a glimpse into the youngster's enthusiasm for these events.

Something happened when Shakespeare was about twelve years old that has never been fully explained. His father stopped attending church and resigned from all his posts. There are a number of possibilities. A few years earlier, John Shakespeare had been accused and fined for 'brogging', or trading wool on the black market. There is also some evidence that he was lending money for interest, a crime in those days. In any case, by 1578, he was obviously short of money. Mary Arden's land was sold along with many of their other holdings. His father never returned to public service. Shakespeare might have left school at about this time. He would have finished at fifteen, as all boys did, but he did not attend university, which would have been a natural next step if his father had remained High Bailiff. Instead, he probably went to work for his father or may have taken up another trade. What is important about this sequence of events is that Shakespeare, throughout his life, sought respectability and property. He applied for and received a coat of arms later in life and owned a great deal of land by the time of his death in 1616. The loss of station and respect is a constant theme in Shakespeare's plays. It would have been difficult for the teenage boy to deal with such a sharp drop in status in a small town. But it may have fuelled the anger and frustration that drives so many of his greatest characters.

The person that most Shakespearean scholars would dearly love to know more about is Shakespeare's wife, Anne. Was she like Juliet, quick-witted and romantic, or was she dreamy and trusting like Desdemona in *Othello*? Or perhaps she was more like Cleopatra. Hopefully, she wasn't anything like Lady Macbeth! Barring the appearance of a lost diary or journal, it is likely that this woman will remain an enigma forever.

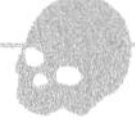

Anne Hathaway

Shakespeare was eighteen and Anne twenty-six when they married in 1582. There is no evidence that this was an arranged marriage. Perhaps they simply met and fell in love. Their first child, Susanna, arrived in 1583, followed two years later by the twins, Hamnet and Judith. There is no evidence that Anne ever lived in or even visited London. Shakespeare's married life, like so much in his story, is likely to remain a mystery.

CHAPTER THREE

THE UPSTART CROW

Investigator:
Sir Richard Topcliffe
Subject:
Thomas Skelton

15 December 1592: The informer, Tom Skelton, is the new court jester following the disgrace and subsequent death of Richard Tarleton. Unlike Tarleton, who was a talented mimic and fencer, Skelton appears to be quite mad, and not terribly funny. He has a reputation for practical jokes that have, on occasion, resulted in the death of the victim. We are interested in the link between William Shakespeare and Christopher 'Kit' Marlowe. Skelton was able to give us a bit of information on the topic.

Topcliffe: How did Will Shakespeare meet Christopher Marlowe?

Skelton: Well, I'll tell you something funny. I think they met the night Tom

Watson killed that fellow Bradley outside the Bishop Inn in Hogs Lane. Will Shakespeare was living in Shoreditch and he must have known that other writer Robert Greene, because that night Will walked into the pub and said, 'Well, it is Roberto Greene, and isn't he a huge hill of flesh, a horse back-breaker, a bed presser…'

Greene laughed and pointed at young Will. 'And you, Sir, are a starveling, an elf skin, a dried neat's tongue, a bull's pizzle…'

They both laughed as Will sat down at the table. In those days, Greene, Nashe, Marlowe and the rest of them were the big men around town, their plays on at all the theatres, people reciting their poems. Shakespeare was a new boy but he had written a play or two. When he wasn't around, Greene and the others laughed about him. You know those fellows and their university degrees. They said he didn't know his Latin or his Greek. They say the same thing about poor old Tom Kyd.

But Marlowe was sitting at the table that night and he kept looking at Shakespeare. Marlowe was probably the best writer of the group, but the way he spoke to young Will, it was as though he thought that Will was even better. Robert Greene was very drunk and told Will that there was no room for uneducated glover's sons and actors at the table. Marlowe drew his sword and placed it under Greene's chin. 'You are a windy fool, Greene. A few years at Cambridge doesn't make one a great poet. You are the best example of that!'

Now Greene didn't like that much, but Marlowe is a dangerous man. You know that, don't you. He's one of yours, isn't he? A spy? Alright, I'll go on. Well Greene just laughed it off, but then a fellow called Bradley, who seemed to know Greene, stood up and challenged Marlowe. Kit told him to sit down but Bradley insisted. I said that I was the court jester and that duels were not permitted. Everyone laughed but Bradley drew his sword and swiped it at Marlowe's ear. He drew a bit of blood and Marlowe jumped to his feet. Bradley must have realised how silly it was to fight Marlowe because he ran outside.

Marlowe followed him and Tom Watson went too. I got up to go out and Will Shakespeare followed me. Outside on the street, the three were arguing. Marlowe was trying to calm Watson down. Bradley had apologised to Marlowe and wanted to leave. Watson was insisting on a fight. Suddenly, Bradley raised his sword and moved towards Watson. Marlowe stepped between them and pushed down Bradley's sword just as Watson came forward and plunged his knife into Bradley's chest. The young man fell to the ground, gurgling. 'A scratch, a scratch, marry 'tis enough. A plague on both your houses,' he said.

I looked at Shakespeare who was watching intently. It was dark but I could see his face, and I swear he was almost smiling.

'Why the devil came you between us?' said Bradley to Marlowe. 'I was hurt beneath your arm. You were holding me back when he charged!'

Shakespeare was nodding. 'The soldiers will come soon, Tom. It is time to depart,' he said.

When I looked again, Shakespeare was gone. Probably back to his writing desk.

HOW SHAKESPEARE REAPPEARED IN HISTORY WHEN SOMEONE MADE FUN OF HIM

One night in 1591, the Devil appeared on stage. It happened in Dulwich, England, during a performance of a play called *Doctor Faustus*. The play is about a man who is so curious about the world that he sells his soul to the Devil in order to understand the secrets of the universe. It is a frightening play, and Satan does make an appearance. Usually he was played by an actor, but, according to the story, on this cold night the real Devil appeared and threatened the famous actor, Edward Allen, who was playing the role of Faustus. Allen was so frightened that he vowed to found a religious school in the town. The College of God's Gift in Dulwich is still standing.

None of this would have been a surprise to the playwright of *Doctor Faustus*. At the time, Christopher Marlowe was the most notorious man in England. In 1589, Marlowe narrowly missed a jail term for his part in a street brawl that left one man dead. His plays were filled with violent scenes and characters who said terrible things about God. Audiences found it difficult to separate the author from his characters. Rumours about Marlowe filled London and he soon came to the attention of the authorities. It was probably about this time that he met Will Shakespeare. They were born in the same year but no one who knew them would have confused the two. Shakespeare avoided drinking as much as possible, and avoided making overtly political or religious statements in his plays and poems. Marlowe was a classic bad boy who loved the spotlight and would do or say anything to keep his name on people's lips. It is sometimes said that Marlowe was Shakespeare's only real rival. Marlowe's fame and writing overshadowed the early part of Shakespeare's life in London, and haunted Shakespeare for the rest of his career.

Marlowe belonged to a group of hard-drinking, fast-living writers known as the University Wits. They were well educated, sophisticated and talented, but not necessarily wealthy. In a society sharply divided along class lines, education represented a possibility for social advancement. Marlowe grew up in circumstances similar to Shakespeare's. His father was a shoemaker and would have expected that his son would follow in the same trade. But for a bright young man there was another option. He won a scholarship to

Cambridge while studying at Kings School, Canterbury. Briefly, he considered becoming a minister, but after a stint as a spy he ended up in London writing poems and plays inspired by the writers he read at university.

The School of Night

The School of Night is the name given to a shadowy group whose members may have included Christopher Marlowe and Walter Raleigh. The name comes from Shakespeare's play *Love's Labour's Lost*. The group was supposedly founded to discuss atheism (the disbelief in God). There is no real evidence that such an organisation ever existed beyond the imaginations of its members' enemies.

By the time Shakespeare arrived in London, the University Wits dominated the theatre scene and were local celebrities. They held court in various pubs, talking and arguing about literature and life. Their views were scandalous, their personal lives were chaotic and most of them died young. But before they died, they managed to produce some fascinating and influential writing.

The unofficial leader of the group was a writer called Robert Greene. Like the other Wits, he came from humble circumstances but had distinguished himself at Cambridge and later Oxford. He had married a wealthy woman and seemed set for a career in medicine before giving it all away for a life in London among the prostitutes and criminal classes. He wrote several plays but was better known for his pamphlets designed to explain the 'low life' of London to the literate members of the middle and upper classes. He took his research seriously, spending much of his time in gambling houses, brothels and pubs.

Greene had left his wife for a prostitute called Emma Ball whose brother was the notorious thief Cutting Ball. Greene had arrived in London a handsome and well-educated gentleman, but by the time Shakespeare arrived in the city, Greene was a sick and bitter alcoholic who spent much of his time raging at other writers, who he considered his inferiors.

By 1592, Shakespeare's career was on the rise and Christopher Marlowe was his only serious rival. Robert Greene was watching from the sidelines and must have seen his own failure magnified by the success of this young man who had not — and this would have infuriated Greene — attended university. It is easy to imagine Greene sitting in his favourite pub surrounded by thieves, con men, hack writers and the occasional spy. He was known to be viciously funny and acknowledged as the best educated and most well-spoken of the group.

Shakespeare, with his country manners and quiet wit, would have been a target for Greene's own cruel sense of humour. It would have been all the more galling then for Greene to see Shakespeare challenging Marlowe, a fellow 'Wit', for the title of London's best playwright.

In the summer of 1592 two events conspired to close the theatres in London. On 11 June, the apprentice of a feltmaker was thrown into prison without any real cause. That afternoon at the Rose Theatre, a large group of apprentices watched a new play and some comedy skits by the clown Will Kempe. Afterwards, they marched to the prison and demanded that their colleague be set free. A riot broke out and the London Council decided that the theatres would be closed until September. They might have closed anyway, because at that time the Plague had returned to the city. No one really knew how plagues spread but there must have been some idea that contact with large groups of people wasn't a good idea. In any case, no one felt much like laughing or being amused by actors when death was everywhere. Shakespeare and his fellow players took the opportunity to tour the countryside. Throughout Shakespeare's career, his livelihood would be threatened by both the Plague and the city council. The theatre was an important part of life in Elizabethan London but, in a society given to paranoia and hysteria, the high profile came at a price.

Robert Greene was left in London. He was broke and, after eating too many pickled herrings with another writer, fatally ill. As he lay on his deathbed covered in lice and fleas, he wrote one last pamphlet in which he attacked everyone he could think of, including William Shakespeare:

> 'Yes trust them not: for there is an upstart Crow, beautified with our feathers, that, with his Tiger's Heart wrapped in a Player's hide, supposes he is as well able to bombast out a blank verse as the best of you: and being an absolute Johannes Factotum, is in his own conceit the only Shakescene in a country.'

Greene saw Shakespeare as an actor who was writing and 'beautifying' plays using the language and ideas of the Wits. There was some truth in this charge. Shakespeare wrote few completely original works. Almost all of his plays were based closely on earlier works by other writers. His most famous plays, including *Hamlet, Romeo and Juliet,* and *King Lear,* were based on plays that were well-known at the time. There is a saying that there are no new plots, and in any case, the quality of Shakespeare's adaptations always rendered the original work redundant. But it isn't difficult to imagine Greene's irritation. The other charge is that he is a 'Johannes Factotum' which translates roughly as 'Jack of All Trades'. Greene and the other Wits saw themselves as scholarly poets who wrote plays, rather than as members of the theatre world. Shakespeare was probably the first major playwright to begin his work in the theatre as an actor. He continued to act throughout his career both in his own plays and those of others. Many critics have suggested that his unique perspective was exactly what gave his plays the edge over writers like Marlowe. But Greene wasn't impressed. The 'Tiger's Heart wrapped in a Player's hide' paraphrases a line from one of Shakespeare's early plays, *Henry VI, Part 2*. Greene is suggesting that Shakespeare is a dangerous man, which in literary terms, he clearly was to the Wits.

It is a nasty passage, filled with spite and snobbery, but it is treasured by historians and scholars because it represents Shakespeare's reappearance in history after seven years. In 1585 he signed the Christening certificate for his twins, Hamnet and Judith, and then promptly disappeared from all public and private records. Seven years later he reappears in Greene's pamphlet. Greene tells us that Shakespeare was an actor and that *Henry VI* had already appeared on the stage. It is also clear that Shakespeare must have been very popular by 1592 to merit such a vicious attack.

No one knows how Shakespeare responded to the attack. Greene died just before the theatres reopened that year. Some scholars believe that Shakespeare's affectionate portrayal of Sir John Falstaff in *Henry IV* and *The Merry Wives of Windsor* may have been based on Robert Greene. Shakespeare may have seen the attack for what it was, the rantings of a sick and unhappy man, and not taken it too seriously. On the other hand, in December of 1592, the publisher of the original pamphlet, Henry Chettle, issued an apology, regretting the libel on Shakespeare. Chettle would have done this at his own expense. Perhaps Shakespeare paid the man a visit and made him an offer he didn't dare refuse.

Sir John Falstaff

Falstaff is one of Shakespeare's best-known creations, a lovable rogue who enjoys food, drink and good times. He stars in *Henry IV, Part 1* and *Part 2* and *The Merry Wives of Windsor*. He was probably first played by the comic actor and clown Will Kempe, and he was popular character from the beginning. Legend has it that Queen Elizabeth insisted Shakespeare write a play about Falstaff in love, so Shakespeare produced *The Merry Wives of Windsor*. There is also a famous opera by Giuseppe Verdi called *Falstaff*, based mainly on *The Merry Wives of Windsor*.

CHAPTER FOUR

A GREAT RECKONING IN A SMALL ROOM

Investigator:
Sir Richard Topcliffe
Subject:
William Kempe

We have been interrogating the clown William Kempe in the aftermath of Christopher Marlowe's death. In the course of the conversation we again tried to establish something about the views of William Shakespeare. Kempe makes much of his 'commonness' but it is clear that he knows more than he is saying.

Topcliffe: Would you say that Shakespeare and Marlowe were close friends?

Kempe: Sure. Marlowe helped him write some of those plays and Shakespeare gave Marlowe the idea for his play about Edward and Gaveston. They talk a lot but they couldn't be more different men. I didn't like that Marlowe fellow at all and I'm not sorry that you boys killed him.

We assure Mr Kempe that we had nothing to do with Marlowe's death.

Kempe: Oh right [*he touches the side of his nose*]. Well, I didn't like him for the simple reason that he didn't like clowns in his plays. Now Shakespeare, well, that boy is one of us. A clown, I mean. He always writes a part for old Will Kempe. He knows that's what people want.

Topcliffe: Did Shakespeare share Marlowe's atheistic views?

Kempe: You're not asking the right question. Will doesn't have views. He's an actor, a clown. Sure, Marlowe took him along to meet those other fellows in the School of Night or what have you. Will listened to Raleigh and the rest talk about demons and the Devil but he couldn't help himself from laughing. Poor old Kit Marlowe didn't know what to do with him. All those gentlemen taking themselves so seriously and young Will laughing at the talk.

At this point we closed the interview and decided to arrest Shakespeare. We found him sitting behind a stage in Surrey, reading a book. We asked him what he was reading. His response was curious and the following conversation unfolded.

Representative of the Queen: 'What do you read, my Lord?'

Shakespeare: 'Words, words, words.'

Rep: 'What is the matter?'

Shakespeare: 'Between who?'

Rep: 'I mean the matter that you read, my Lord.'

Shakespeare: 'Oh, it is all slanders, Sir. It says that poets are murdered and government men are corrupt. I will say, Sir, that I have found these slanders most amusing as they are so clearly untrue.'

He laughed maniacally and somehow caused the book to vanish from sight, at which point the Representative of the Queen chose to depart. Note: There seems to be some method in Master Shakespeare's madness. Also, he may have magic powers.

We brought Will Kempe in again for further questioning. He was very amused by Will Shakespeare's response.

Kempe: Oh ho, he is witty fellow, indeed, but no danger to you men. Will Shakespeare is not atheist or secret Catholic. He is a glovemaker's son from Stratford and he wants to be a gentleman. He might have had a lark with your interrogators but you've frightened him now. Marlowe was his friend. We're all a bit scared. When they start killing poets, can clowns be far behind?

Another unsatisfactory interview on the subject of Will Shakespeare. It is becoming increasingly clear that there is more to the story. Shakespeare must be planning something. No one so clever could simply be writing plays.

HOW SHAKESPEARE LOST HIS MENTOR AND BECAME THE GREATEST WRITER IN HISTORY

The murder of Christopher Marlowe remains one of history's great unexplained crimes. It is unexplained rather than unsolved because there was no question about who killed him. Ingram Frizer was pardoned by the Queen for the killing two weeks after it happened. The two other men, Robert Poley and Nicholas Skeres, were arrested but not charged. There is no question about *how* he died. It is the *why* that continues to vex historians.

On the surface, it seems very straightforward. Marlowe, Frizer, Poley and Skeres spent the day drinking at Mistress Bull's Tavern in Deptford, in East London. After a long day, the three men quarrelled about the bill. Marlowe was not a man to back down, and a fight broke out. At some point, Ingram Frizer pulled out a dagger and pushed it into Marlowe's eye. The blade would have gone into his brain and killed him very quickly.

Nobody would have been particularly surprised that Marlowe died in a bar brawl. He had already narrowly escaped a murder charge three years earlier and he was well-known to be quick to quarrel. Marlowe lived his life like a man running out of time. His most famous play, *Doctor Faustus,* was about a man who sold his soul so that he could see the world and know everything. Marlowe had come to London as one of the University Wits and had enormous success as a playwright and poet. But like many of the other Wits he died young. For someone of his temperament, dying in an argument over a few shillings was almost fitting. Except, it wasn't the real reason he was killed.

Christopher Marlowe was murdered, or rather executed, by the forces that had once employed him. Although Marlowe attended Cambridge, it would seem that most of his time was spent in France and Holland, spying on the various English Catholic communities that resided there. England was at war with Spain throughout this period and the English authorities regarded the English Catholics living in the Netherlands as enemies. To meet this threat, an enormous spy network evolved throughout England and Europe. One of the Queen's favourites, Francis Walsingham, presided over much of the espionage operations, but all the Queen's favourites ran their own investigations. There was no clear line of command and no central power. The Queen's favourites worked against each other, and England was a hotbed of rumours, plots and secret meetings. Marlowe slipped into one of the cracks between two powerful favourites, and died as a result.

Marlowe worked directly for Walsingham and carried out a number of missions while he was supposed to be studying. There is no real evidence about the nature of these missions but it can be assumed that he posed as a theology student who intended to become a Catholic priest. He would have lived among the English Catholics somewhere in Northern Europe, possibly Rheims in France, and listened carefully for any talk of plots against the Queen. His regular reports must have been well received and he must have proved a useful spy. When he finished at Cambridge, the university initially refused to grant him a degree because of his poor attendance. It would have been hard to attend classes while spying in France. Very quickly however, the degree was awarded and special mention was made of his service to Her Majesty. Marlowe had powerful friends, but in the murky world of spies, friends can quickly become enemies.

It is not clear whether Marlowe continued to do intelligence work after arriving in London and becoming a successful playwright and poet. Walsingham and his successor Lord Burleigh seemed to focus their attentions on the Catholic threat in England and abroad. Other figures close to the Queen, such as Sir Robert Cecil, were focused on the puritans (an extremist protestant group in England), and the rise of atheism. Marlowe became associated with atheism through statements made by characters in his plays and statements attributed to him by others. Whether this was just another disguise or cover is difficult to say. Marlowe was connected to a group known as the School of Night, that was rumoured to include, among other influential members, Sir Walter Raleigh. The group was supposedly involved in witchcraft and Satanic rituals. If this was true, then the man who wrote *Doctor Faustus* would have certainly been approached to join. But did he go as a spy or because he was sincerely interested in the discussions?

English Catholics in Europe: A Threat from Abroad.
When Elizabeth became Queen she returned England to Protestantism. Some English Catholics feared persecution and fled to the remaining Catholic countries in Europe, such as France and Spain. These people were perceived as enemies of Queen Elizabeth and regarded with suspicion by her government. This fear was not completely irrational, as the restoration of the Catholic Church in England was certainly the goal of some members of these communities.

Protestants versus Catholics

The issue that dominated Shakespeare's England was religion. The Queen's father, Henry VIII, had broken away from the Roman Catholic Church with the Act of Supremacy (1534), which made him the absolute head of the Church of England. But many people in England remained loyal to the Pope and the Catholic Church. Henry persecuted Catholics ruthlessly and this was continued by his son Edward VI. When Elizabeth's half-sister Mary became Queen, the country reverted to Catholicism and Protestants (those loyal to the Church of England) were persecuted. These divisions created a virtual civil war in England. Elizabeth re-established the Church of England and the Act of Supremacy that made her the head of the church. The modern Queen, Elizabeth II, remains the head of the Protestant Church.

Shakespeare grew up in the early years of Elizabeth's reign while England trod the slow path back to stability. Catholics were tolerated as long as they kept their views to themselves, but were discriminated against and ran the risk of being accused of treason. Shakespeare's plays resonate with divisions, real and imagined. *Romeo and Juliet* in particular, with its 'two houses, both alike', can be seen as an appeal for tolerance. Shakespeare's own religious views are a matter of controversy. Recent biographers suggest he was a secret Catholic, though it seems more likely that this cautious man would not have risked his career in that way.

The events leading to Marlowe's death are dramatic enough to suggest that it was more than just a disagreement about the bill. In early 1593, someone began to post notices all over London about Belgian and Dutch Protestant immigrants who had recently arrived in the city. The notices were libellous and racist. They were all signed 'Tamburlaine', which was the title character of one of Marlowe's most popular plays. Soon after the notices went up, Marlowe was arrested and held for two days by the Privy Council. He was set free but asked to return for further questioning. In the meantime, his friend and sometime roommate Thomas Kyd was arrested. Kyd, a playwright, was tortured and questioned about atheistic literature found in his rooms. He swore that it belonged to Marlowe. The Privy Council recalled Marlowe and told him to report to them daily. It was clear that he would soon undergo the same treatment as Kyd. Or was it? Perhaps this was all part of a plot to catch a more important figure, possibly Raleigh.

Marlowe's drinking companions on the last day of his life were all shadowy figures connected in some way to the Walsingham family. Marlowe's death may have been a matter of silencing someone with too much information. The Walsingham family may have decided that it was too risky to have Marlowe questioned by the Privy Council. Or perhaps they decided that he was actually working for them and spying on his former employers. We will probably never know exactly why Marlowe died, but it is clear that it was more than a question of splitting the bill.

Francis Walsingham

Sir Francis Walsingham was the Spymaster of the Elizabethan era. To protect England from a Spanish invasion or Catholic uprising, he employed spies all over Europe. He infiltrated English Catholic communities with false converts like the young Christopher Marlowe. It was Sir Francis who discovered the plot to replace Elizabeth with her cousin Mary, Queen of Scots.

Walter Raleigh

Sir Walter is one of the most colourful figures in English history. He is credited with planting the first potato in Ireland, founding the first English colony in North America and bringing tobacco to Europe. He was a favourite of Queen Elizabeth. He also wrote poetry and had many contacts among writers. He was executed in 1618 following a disastrous journey to South America in search of the fabled city of El Dorado.

Shakespeare makes several references to Marlowe's death in *As You Like It*, a play that was first staged several years after the murder. The clown Touchstone says that when a man's writing is misunderstood, 'it strikes a man more dead than a great reckoning in a little room.' A 'reckoning' is an old term for a bill. Elsewhere in the play he refers to a 'dead shepherd' and quotes one of Marlowe's famous lines about 'the face that launched a thousand ships'. One of Marlowe's most famous poems was called *The Passionate Shepherd to His Love*. When Marlowe died, he and Shakespeare were by far the two most popular playwrights in London. Marlowe's influence is evident in many of Shakespeare's early plays and they may have even collaborated on some scenes in the *Henry VI* plays.

Marlowe and Shakespeare were very different men. Marlowe was hard-living, with all kinds of connections, a shadowy past and a bad temper. Shakespeare seems to have worked hard to avoid any connection with the forces that killed his colleague. Marlowe's death would have been a warning to him and it was one that he seems to have heeded. Whatever Shakespeare's opinions were on politics and religion, he successfully buried them. His lack of a university education, so colourfully noted by Robert Greene, may have been an advantage. As an actor, rather than a poet, his world was the theatre. He came from Stratford without powerful connections and survived the dangerous world of the factions that sprang up around Queen Elizabeth.

Marlowe's death also had an effect on Shakespeare's plays. After Marlowe was killed, Shakespeare began to develop his own voice. *Romeo and Juliet,* with the Marlowe-like character Mercutio, was a departure from the kinds of plays that he had previously written. He may have lost a friend, but he had also lost his only serious competitor on the London stage. No longer did he feel compelled to imitate or better the other playwright's stories. He would remain the pre-eminent playwright in London for the rest of his life.

CHAPTER FIVE

SORROWS IN BATTALIONS

Investigator:
Sir Richard Topcliffe
Subject:
William Kempe

The subject of this interview is the clown Will Kempe. He is a reliable informant and has been helping us to collect data on Will Shakespeare, an actor and playwright, who is one of the best-known figures in the London theatre world. So far we have gathered very little that might help us to gain some advantage over Shakespeare should we need to question him. This excerpt deals with the arrest of another playwright, Ben Jonson.

Topcliffe: Was Shakespeare distressed at Jonson's arrest? Would he not have been pleased that yet another rival was out of the way?

Kempe: Oh no, not Will. He was terribly upset about Marlowe's murder, ahem, death and when he heard about Ben, he was most upset.

Topcliffe: How do you know?

Kempe: Will was playing a role in Ben's play when it happened. Just before the play started, Gabriel Spencer was shouting at Ben outside the theatre. We all went out to see what the noise was about and found Gabriel with his hands around Ben's neck. Spencer was mad. A few years ago he killed Thomas Leake with a rapier. I was there and saw it. We were outside a tavern in Cheapside and Leake came up to Gabriel with a large candlestick. He claimed that he was owed money or something. Gabriel didn't hesitate. He drew his rapier and drove it through Leake's chest. We were all there and said it was self-defence, but I wasn't so sure.

Anyway, here's Gabriel choking poor Ben. Shakespeare was begging Gabriel to let him go, but Gabe was so angry that he couldn't hear. I was going to intervene but Shakespeare stopped me. Breaking up these sorts of matters can be dangerous, he said. Soon there was a big crowd and everyone was shouting. Gabriel let go of Ben and started to walk away but by this time Ben was furious. He pulled out his dagger and yelled to Gabriel. Gabe turned around just in time to see Ben sticking the dagger into his chest. Gabriel died with his eyes fixed on Ben.

Shakespeare was standing not two arms length from them, shaking his head. 'This has got to stop,' says he. Ben turned and ran away, leaving the cast of his new play without two of its principal actors. We did the show anyway but it wasn't a great performance. Afterwards, when we came out, Gabriel was still lying on the street. I went and found his brother who took away the body.

Ben was arrested that night and all of the witnesses said that the fight was over when he stabbed poor Gabe. There was nothing anyone could do for Ben. He was going to be hanged.

I came across Shakespeare a few nights later in the Mermaid Tavern with a few actors. Will is no drinker and I was surprised to see him there. He was a bit drunk. 'First Kit Marlowe, then my poor son Hamnet, now Ben,' he kept saying. Will was hit pretty hard when his son died but he hadn't mentioned it much lately. Ben was a bit like a younger brother to Will, so his impending death must have brought back some memories. And of Marlowe too, who was like a big brother to Will. One of the actors was trying to cheer him up. 'Hey Will, maybe you can find some law to save him, like in that play about the money lender and his daughter,' the actor said. In case you don't know it, Sir, *The Merchant of Venice* is a play about a man who borrows money and offers a pound of his own flesh as security. When he can't pay, the money lender wants his pound of flesh. A lawyer, who is really a girl in disguise — you know how much Will loves that idea — points out that the law protects its citizens from such threats and the money lender loses everything.

Will looked up at the actor for a second, and then jumped up and was gone. The rest of us laughed about it and raised our glasses to Ben, who was soon to be swinging.

A few days later I went to Will's rooms in Shoreditch and found him pouring over a large book that he had borrowed from a friend who had studied law at Cambridge.

'I've got the solution, clown Kempe,' says Will.

'Well, what is it?'

'When Henry II was after Thomas Beckett,' he says, and I knew this was going to be long story, 'Beckett tried to tell the King he had no power over priests. Henry wasn't happy about this and had him killed at Canterbury—'

'Yes, alright, Will, write a play about it. Call it *Murder In The Cathedral* or whatever, but what does any of this have to do with our Ben?'

'Well, after he killed Beckett and everyone was so angry, he was forced to make a law that made clergymen exempt from anything but church law. To prove that you were a clergyman, you had to read a Psalm in Latin from the page. The wonderful thing is, clown, it is still a provision in our law today!'

'Great news, Will, but our Ben is definitely not a clergyman.'

'No matter. It is a provision in the law and therefore applies to everyone who can read Latin.'

At that, Will Shakespeare went marching off to Newgate to let Ben know. I didn't hold out much hope until a few weeks later when Ben came into the Mermaid with a large 'T' branded on his thumb.

'What happened?' I asked.

'Well, they didn't hang me but I have a very sore thumb. Our Will didn't read the fine print. You can only use the provision once and they brand your finger just in case you try it again.'

HOW THINGS WENT FROM BAD TO WORSE TO BETTER FOR WILLIAM SHAKESPEARE

In August 1596, William Shakespeare's only son, Hamnet, died in Stratford. He was eleven years old and had grown up with his twin sister Judith, his older sister Susanna and his mother Anne. His father was present at his christening in 1585 but probably wasn't around much as he was growing up. No one knows whether or not Shakespeare attended the funeral on 11 August. Communications were difficult in those days and travel was expensive, slow and often dangerous. Still, it must have been a terrible blow to the playwright. It was not uncommon for families to lose children. Shakespeare's own sister Anne had died at age nine, when Shakespeare was fifteen. Surviving into adulthood was something of an achievement in the period, and parents had to be prepared for the very real possibility that they might lose their children.

But it still would have been a very sad occasion, and there is a passage in a play *King John*, written soon after Hamnet's death, that might give some clues as to Shakespeare's emotional state at the time. The lines are delivered by Constance, the mother of a small boy who has died:

Grief fills the room up of my absent child,
Lies in his bed, walks up and down with me,
Puts on his pretty looks, repeats his words,
Remembers me of all his gracious parts,
Stuffs out his vacant garments with his form.

There is something in those lines that suggests real grief rather than a stagey show of tears. Earlier, she says 'That we shall see and know our friends in heaven: If that be true, I shall see my boy again.' They are sad lines, and scholars have long sensed something of Shakespeare's loss in them.

Fathers and sons figure prominently in a number of the plays that followed Hamnet's death. *Henry IV, Part 1* and *Part 2*, are primarily concerned with the relationship between the King and his tearaway son Hal. *Hamlet*, whose name is oddly similar to Shakespeare's son, deals with a child's responsibility to a dead father. There is also *Twelfth Night*, which features twins. One of the twins is thought to be dead but returns. Shakespeare wrote to please his audiences; the idea of the self-conscious writer who talks about himself in every work is a very modern one. However, there are patterns in the plays that do seem to match some of what is known about Shakespeare's life. The loss of an only son, particularly when his wife Anne was past the age where she could have more children, would have been devastating to a man who seems to have been so committed to becoming a gentleman. He would have regarded his life's work as founding a line of Shakespeares who would cherish his memory. With Hamnet's death, this became impossible.

A year later in the summer of 1597, an incident occurred that nearly finished off the London theatre scene and Shakespeare's livelihood for good. Thomas Nashe, one of the last of the University Wits, and an up-and-coming playwright named Ben Jonson, wrote a play. Called *The Isle of Dogs*, the play was performed by Lord Pembroke's Men at the Swan Theatre. The title of the now lost play referred to a place on the Thames where sewage sometimes built up and gave off a terrible smell. However, it was also home to the place where the powerful Privy Council sometimes met. Nashe and Jonson used this double meaning as a title for a play that made fun of many important public figures, including the Queen. As Shakespeare was to learn, plays were taken very seriously. The Privy Council did not see the funny side of the play and it was closed almost at once. Warrants for the arrest of the authors were issued and Thomas Nashe fled from London. Ben Jonson was interrogated by the fearsome Sir Richard Topcliffe and placed in a cell with an informer named Robert Poley, the shadowy figure who was present when Christopher Marlowe was murdered. The Privy Council declared war on the local theatres. An order was given that all such buildings should be 'plucked down'. Fortunately, it was never carried out. Too many nobles, including the Queen, were fans of the entertainment provided by the plays. The matter slowly faded away and Ben Jonson was released from prison in October 1597.

The Privy Council

The Privy Council met several times a week to advise the Queen and to make decisions concerning the day-to-day running of the country. It was made up of about twenty of the most powerful men in the country as chosen by the Queen. The Privy Council was often involved in questioning people accused of treason and was much feared. Needless to say, the council was a hotbed of shifting loyalties. Shakespeare's interest in the personal dimension of politics may have been inspired by the figures that surrounded the Queen.

However, all of the theatres were closed for most of the summer for the second time in five years. Shakespeare, who never courted controversy, must have been frustrated by the loss of revenue and the increasingly bad reputation of the theatres, actors and playwrights. His own plays up until this point had usually included characters designed to reflect the rough-and-tumble nature of the London streets. There are plenty of 'low life' moments in his early plays and plenty of space for a comedian like Will Kempe to improvise, perhaps on timely subjects. At the close of the 1590s, Shakespeare seemed to be moving away from those scenes and any possibility for misinterpretation. It is hardly surprising in the wake of Marlowe's death and another incident that occurred in 1598.

Ben Jonson

Ben Jonson was a friend and rival of Shakespeare. He is best known for plays like *Volpone* and *The Alchemist*. Jonson was an outspoken and controversial figure who often annoyed the authorities with his plays.

Ben Jonson had not been out of prison for a year when he became involved in an argument with Gabriel Spencer, an actor in the Admiral's Men theatre company. Spencer was a rising young talent but the previous year had killed a man who had attacked him with a candlestick. No one knows how the quarrel between Jonson and Spencer started, but it finished when Ben Jonson killed Spencer with a dagger. Once again he was arrested but this time he was taken to the frightening Newgate prison and sentenced to hang. At the time, his play *Every Man In His Humour* was playing in London. Shakespeare may have been acting in it and would have surely been distressed at the idea of a fellow playwright being executed.

Jonson escaped death in a manner that sounds like something Shakespeare might have written. He discovered a provision in English law that dated back to the twelfth century and was designed to protect clergymen from prosecution under anything but church law. To fulfil what was called the 'benefit of the clergy', a person had to read a section of the Bible. That might sound straightforward, but the Bible was not translated into English until much later, and generally only clergymen could read Latin. Usually the reading was the appropriate Psalm 50, which includes the lines *Miserere mei, Deus, secundum misericordiam tuam.* (O God, have mercy upon me, according to thine heartfelt mercifulness). People in the Middle Ages who were illiterate would simply memorise the whole psalm, and it soon became known as the 'neck verse'. Ben Jonson didn't have to memorise it as he was quite literate in several languages. He escaped hanging but was branded with a 'T' on his left thumb. The brand meant that he had used the benefit of the clergy once but would not be able to do so again. Shakespeare may have found this episode amusing but he must have also looked forward to a period where playwrights avoided such scenes entirely.

The law itself lasted in England until 1827 when it was abolished by Parliament. It was a provision in American law until shortly after the revolution. It remained on the books in some American states, and it was invoked once in South Carolina in the 1850s. There is a strong possibility that in states where no one ever bothered to abolish the law it may still be possible to save one's life simply by reading.

CHAPTER SIX

THE NINE DAY WONDER

Investigator:
Sir Richard Topcliffe
Subject:
William Kempe

This is a transcript of an interview with Will Kempe, a well-known clown. Until recently he was an actor with the Lord Chamberlain's Men theatre company. Kempe was an excellent source of information on Will Shakespeare, though we remain perplexed as to his motives. His departure from the company is a disappointing development.

Topcliffe: You say that Will Shakespeare stopped writing parts for you because he wanted to be a gentleman. What do you mean?

Kempe: It's simple — he was scared, wasn't he. He doesn't want any more of the street-life. He's tired of losing half his audience to Harry Hunks and the other bears. Will says the future of the theatre is with a better sort of person. That's what Marlowe thought too, but he got killed arguing over the bill, didn't he? *[subject winks — noted]*. Anyway, it's all Falstaff's fault, isn't it.

Topcliffe: Who is Falstaff?

Kempe: Me. Well, he's the character in the play. See, Will wrote this very serious play about King Henry IV and his son. Wrote two plays about them in fact. Well, he wrote this part for me, a character called Sir John Falstaff. Now, in the play this Falstaff is a friend of young Prince Hal, and he is a bad influence on him. Falstaff is a bit of a drinker, a bit of a thief, and likes a certain type of lady. But he has a good heart, right. Maybe Will was thinking of poor Bob Greene?
I don't know. So I'm playing Falstaff to the hilt, throwing in a few extra lines here and there, and the audience loves it. But while King Henry is having a serious talk with his son Hal, the groundlings are yelling, 'Falstaff, Falstaff!' As soon as I'm back on stage, they're happy again so I think I had better keep going. I drag my scene out, and introduce a wee jig into the middle. When King Henry comes back out, people start leaving. No one wants to hear it. They want Falstaff.

You might imagine that our Will was not pleased.

'Stick to your lines, clown,' says he.

'But they don't want your old King, they want Will Kempe,' I said.

Dick Burbage, the actor who plays the King, is standing nearby and pulls out his dagger. 'I'm going to kill him Will,' he says. 'I'm going to kill the clown.'

Will Shakespeare, the cheeky boy, says, 'Not yet, Dick.' Not yet?

But as usual I have the last laugh, for it turns out that the Queen herself is quite taken with old Falstaff and wants Will to write a play about Falstaff in love. Well, what could he do? He writes this play, *The Merry Wives of Windsor,* and it is complete rubbish. I try to fix it up with some jokes but Will gets angry again. I say, 'Hey Will, watch the audience. This is the worst thing you have ever written and the only bits that the audience are enjoying are the parts I'm making up on the spot.'

Meanwhile, everyone is still suffering because of Ben and Tom's play about the dogs. Shakespeare starts to talk about writing gentleman plays for gentleman. I tell him that if he writes one more play like *The Merry Wives*, he'll be writing parts for Harry Hunks. He says that when he wants to hear from the clown, he'll ring a bell.

Then he killed me.

Topcliffe: What?

Kempe: That's right. He killed me. I should have known I was in trouble. At the end of the second part of *Henry IV*, he had me say the epilogue. I said something like, 'Our humble author will continue the story with Sir John in it.' The audience was cheering and hollering so they missed the next part: 'Where, for anything I know, Falstaff shall die of a sweat — unless already a' be killed with your hard opinions.' Now what does that mean? It was Shakespeare's hard opinion that killed Sir John Falstaff. Then I started thinking about something else that happens in the play. Just near the end, Falstaff approaches Prince Hal who is now the King. The new King Harry says, 'I know thee not old man. Fall to thy prayers. How ill white hairs become a fool and jester.' He was saying that I was too old to be a clown! Oh, Will Shakespeare is a nasty one.

Topcliffe: Wasn't there a play about King Henry V?

Kempe: Sure, and when it started everyone was calling for Falstaff, but he never arrives. Then one of the characters says 'Falstaff is dead,' and that is the end of it. The play is alright but I think he wrote the whole thing just to get rid of Will Kempe.

Topcliffe: So you decided to dance across the country?

Kempe: Sure, who wants to hear about old kings anyway? The people, the real people, love old Will Kempe and they always will.

The subject then outlined his plan to Morris dance his way to Italy. It would seem that he has nothing left to tell us about Will Shakespeare. The playwright's motives remain elusive to us and we shall have to find a new informant.

HOW SHAKESPEARE LOST A CLOWN AND BECAME A BETTER WRITER

In the spring of 1599, Shakespeare's clown Will Kempe decided to sell his shares in the Lord Chamberlain's Men theatre company and dance across the country. No one knows for sure why Kempe, for whom Shakespeare created some of his best-known characters, would give up a solid source of income to embark on what amounted to a publicity stunt.

The dance he chose to perform was the Morris. The dance involves rhythmic turns to music played by a pipe and drum combination. It was by far the most popular dance of the period and Kempe was a known master. Before he began, he took bets on whether or not he would finish. Though he called it the 'Nine Day Wonder', it actually took several weeks. He was accompanied by a musician, as well as a servant and his 'manager'. He had many adventures along the way, including affairs with local girls and run-ins with innkeepers. It is likely that much of the trip was fuelled by strong ale. Kempe was also known for his ability to leap very high and over great distances. He partly financed the trip with bets and competitions based on great jumps along the way. When he finished, he wrote a popular book about his experiences called *Will Kempe's Nine Day Wonder*. The book was produced partly to convince people that he had in fact completed the trip.

The Theatre Companies

In Shakespeare's time, actors, musicians and other performers were regarded with some suspicion by the authorities. As a way of maintaining some control over the entertainment world, certain nobles were given a licence to become patrons of groups of players. The Lord Chamberlain became responsible for Shakespeare's company and provided them with a name. The name gave them status but also meant that they were answerable to their patron. The patron did not necessarily provide financial support. Other companies at the time included the Admiral's Men and Lord Chandos's Men.

The stunt made a famous man even more famous. Dancing across the country had a novelty value and celebratory spirit that caught the public imagination.

Kempe's roles in Shakespeare's plays suggest that he enjoyed the company of common people and had little interest in social climbing of any kind. The Nine Day Wonder may have been a way for him to reconnect with the kind of people who appreciated his talents as tastes began to change in London.

Shakespeare mentions *The Nine Day Wonder* by name in *As You Like It,* a play that featured his new clown Robert Armin. With the publication of his book, Will Kempe would have been in demand at festivals all over the country. A year later he attempted to Morris dance to Italy. The novelty value was gone, and, outside of England, the dance would have lost something of its context. Kempe returned to England and began to work again with various theatre companies.

By Shakespeare's time, clowns had a long history in England. English theatre grew out of the rituals surrounding the festivals that took place in villages and towns in the Middle Ages. Christmas festivals often featured a 'Lord of Misrule', who encouraged people to have fun during the holiday. In a very early English play called *Mankind* that appeared in the late 1400s, a character similar to 'Misrule', called 'Mischief', appeared as a foil to the character 'Mercy'. As this character provided the drama and humour that drove the story, he became an audience favourite. In the Tudor period at the beginning of the 1500s, a character called

'Vice' became a feature of plays performed at festivals. This character became central to these plays and set the mould for the charismatic and wickedly funny bad guy that can still engage audiences. Think about the Joker's place in *Batman* comics and movies. Batman may be the hero, but audiences love the Joker.

The other tradition that established the role of the clown in Shakespeare's plays was the medieval fool, or jester. The word fool comes from the Latin 'follis' which means 'bag of wind'. Traditionally, the court jester or fool had the job of entertaining the monarch and being able to do so with some freedom. The fool could make fun of the king or queen without losing his head. Thus, the fool was not part of the court hierarchy. The joker in a deck of cards still has no assigned value.

By Shakespeare's time, the role of the company's clown was to perform jigs at the end of a play. A jig was a dance based skit or series of skits. The clown would do tricks like juggling and tumbling while acting out a short and often bawdy story. Some playwrights, like Christopher Marlowe, were actively involved in moving away from this tradition. At the beginning of his play, *Tamburlaine,* Marlowe promises to lead his audience away, 'From jigging veins of rhyming mother-wits / and such conceits as clownage keeps in pay.' Shakespeare did not entirely agree. He saw the powerful effect that these clowns had on the audience and began to incorporate them into the actual plays. Although the title role in *Richard III* would not have been played by the company clown, the character Richard is similar to 'Vice' and 'Mischief' in a way that the audience would have understood. Shakespeare's early plays featured parts written specifically for Will Kempe. Peter in *Romeo and Juliet* and the hapless policeman Dogberry in *Much Ado About Nothing* are roles for the kind of comedy that would have suited Kempe. His most famous role, however, was Falstaff in *Henry IV, Part 1* and *Part 2*. To say he steals the show is an understatement. Falstaff *is* the show. He was the most popular character that Shakespeare created in his time, and was popular even with the Queen.

Eventually, even Shakespeare decided that he had had enough of jig making clowns. *Henry V* did not feature Falstaff, except to report his sad death. By 1599, Shakespeare's company was performing *Julius Caesar*, a play with no role for a clown. Later that year, Hamlet advises a group of travelling actors to 'let those that play your clowns speak no more than is set down for them'. From these lines, it would seem that there was some friction between the natural comedian who improvised and interacted with the audience and the playwright who was on the verge of writing his most important works. The two had served each other well, so it is sad that it ended badly. Kempe refers to 'Shakerags' as one of his enemies in his book and he never again acted in a Shakespeare play. He died of the Plague in 1603. In the parish records book is an epitaph he would have appreciated: Will Kempe, a man.

Kempe's departure from Shakespeare's company, the Lord Chamberlain's Men, was very significant. His replacement Robert Armin was a very different type of clown. Where Kempe's slapstick style had appealed to the common man, Armin was a much darker and cynical type of comedian. Shakespeare's plays grew darker as well, and the result was a series of masterpieces including *Hamlet, Macbeth, King Lear* and *Othello*.

The Lord Chamberlain's Men

This is the theatre company that Shakespeare belonged to for most of his career. It began in 1594 and continued until 1603 when it became known as the King's Men. Shakespeare's plays made up most of the repertoire, though they also performed plays by other playwrights. They performed in The Theatre, which was one of the original playhouses in London. They moved to the nearby Curtain Theatre for a time until 1599, when they built the Globe Theatre.

CHAPTER SEVEN

THE DISTRACTED GLOBE

Investigator:
Sir Richard Topcliffe
Subject:
Robert Armin

This transcript is part of an interview with Robert Armin, who has recently joined the Lord Chamberlain's Men. He has replaced Will Kempe as the company clown, and we hope that he will be able to provide more substantial information than his predecessor. It should be noted that Robert Armin is a very serious sort of clown.

Topcliffe: Tell us about Will Shakespeare.

Armin: He's a man.

Topcliffe: No more than that?

Armin: No, he seems to be only a man.

Topcliffe: A certain Mr Giles Allen says that he is a thief and that he has stolen a theatre?

Armin: Perhaps he is more than a man after all. I mean, to steal an entire theatre…

Topcliffe: Come now, Mr Armin. We don't have to remind you that we retain certain documents attributed to you that deny the existence of—

Armin: Yes, yes, I know, youthful high spirits, atheism and all that. Alright, what can I tell you?

Topcliffe: About Shakespeare's role in the theft of Mr Allen's theatre, please.

Armin: Yes, well, a few nights after Christmas last year, Dick Burbage and Will called a meeting of the Lord Chamberlain's Men and the other shareholders in the Curtain Theatre. Will Kempe was still the company clown but Burbage and Shakespeare had decided that I would replace him, so I was invited along. Poor old Will Kempe. When I arrived, he was dancing around the stage.

'Bob Arm-in, Will Kempe out,' he sang while everyone looked down at their shoes.

Will and Dick Burbage stood on the stage and spoke to the group. It wasn't only shareholders but also a few master builders with their apprentices. There were also a number of cony-catchers and cut-purses, local riff-raff and the like.

'The land belongs to Giles Allen,' said Will. 'But the theatre belongs to us.'

I realised that he was talking about The Theatre in Shoreditch, where I had seen so many of Will's plays. I also saw a few of Marlowe's plays there. Is it true that you fellows murdered him? Alright, wrong question. Anyway, Will carried on:

'We will dismantle The Theatre and build it again in Southwark, on the other side of the Thames.'

Everyone started laughing. Will Kempe did a backflip onto his hands.

'Are you the magician now? Will The Theatre float through the air as you hold it in your spell? Arise, great Theatre, to Southwark. The bears await!'

'Perhaps, clown,' said Will, 'one of your jigs might be the opiate to put The Theatre to sleep while I move it?'

The group roared. I might say here that Will Shakespeare would have been the greatest fool in English history, had he not become such a serious actor and playwright. No one would dare challenge Will Kempe in this manner.

'A speech from *The Merry Wives of Windsor* might kill it off altogether,' said Will Kempe.

The audience all turned to see if Shakespeare would return fire.

'Ah, sweet death. Sans eyes, sans ears and most mercifully, sans Kempe.'

Applause broke out until Dick Burbage hushed everyone.

'Enough of this, we are losing time. We have our weapons and our tools. Tonight we shall dismantle and remove what is ours.'

'Ain't then it a bit of trespassing?' Asked a toothless fellow, who would probably hang if he was caught on someone else's land.

'Our Theatre occupies the entirety of Allen's precious land. We will leave the foundations and no one will set foot on the land itself,' said Will.

Topcliffe: What happened?

Armin: It was a cold night; you could see people's breath in the torchlight as they worked. The master builders and their apprentices climbed the building and began to lift large planks from the roof. Nearby stood the rest of us, watching and chatting. Eventually, people began to come out of their houses, sleepy-eyed and looking worried. An old man addressed me:

'What army is this? Are you Essex's rabble, come to depose our glorious Queen?'

'No, old man,' I said. 'What a foolish notion. This is the Lord Chamberlain's Men.'

'Is he coming to depose our glorious Queen?'

'No, no. We are the players. The acting company.'

'But you are so well-armed?'

'Props, my friend. There is no better stocked armoury in London than the Curtain Theatre. Battle scenes, you understand. No wooden swords for this company.'

'I shall certainly attend a performance soon,' said the old man.

'Good fellow,' said I.

It wasn't long before some of Giles Allen's family appeared.

'You'll swing for this!' shrieked Allen's mother. 'The whole cony-catching lot of you! You're all rascals, eaters of broken meats, base, proud, shallow, beggarly, three-suited, hundred pound, filthy worsted-stocking knaves; lily-livered, action taking, glass gazing, super-serviceable rogues; one-trunk inheriting—'

'Enough!' shouted an apprentice boy as he chased her away with an axe.

We could still hear her insults and jibes when her son's lawyer appeared. They addressed Will Shakespeare.

'You are trespassing, Sir.'

'I am not,' said Will.

'Your men are on Mr Allen's property.'

'They are certainly not *on* his property. They are above it. Does a bird trespass on Her Majesty's property when it flies over Whitechapel?'

Topcliffe: Will Shakespeare has a finely tuned ear for the law. Does he believe himself to be above it? What do you think, Mr Armin?

Armin: No, I think Will would acknowledge that he is not above the law but squarely on it. Or under it. Remember, Mr Allen tried to prosecute his case unsuccessfully. Nobody trespassed. Nothing was stolen. Will says that the law 'is an ass'. He may be right.

Topcliffe: Mr Shakespeare plays a dangerous game.

HOW SHAKESPEARE AND HIS FRIENDS STOLE A THEATRE

Three days after Christmas in 1598, Will Shakespeare and some of his fellow actors stole a theatre. Along with some well-armed friends, the met up on a frosty winter night, dismantled The Theatre as it was imaginatively known, and took it across the Thames.

The Theatre in Shoreditch was one of the oldest venues for plays in London. All of Marlowe and Shakespeare's early works had been staged there. But in 1597, the Lord Chamberlain's Men had fallen out with the landlord Giles Allen over the rent and had stopped using the venue. Allen was a puritan (a particularly strict religious group) and had never been happy about having a theatre on his land. He gave notice to the company, who were forced to quickly relocate to the nearby Curtain Theatre. The first plan had been to build a new theatre in an old monastery in the Blackfriars area of London. The company invested a great deal of money into renovations, but lost it all when the residents of the neighbourhood decided that a theatre would only bring noise and the wrong sort of people.

As the new year, 1599, loomed, the company was in serious financial trouble. They made a new but slightly risky plan. Legally, the land on which The Theatre stood belonged to Giles Allen. The lease had expired and Allen had decided to use the building as a warehouse. But it wasn't his building. It belonged to the Lord Chamberlain's Men.

The company took out an inexpensive lease on a piece of property in Southwark on the other side of the Thames. The new site was close to the Rose Theatre, which housed their main rivals, the Admiral's Men. It was also near several bear baiting venues. It was, however, not a particularly promising piece of land. In fact, so close was it to the Thames that elaborate foundations had to be built to ensure that the new theatre did not sink into the marshy land beneath it. This proved expensive, as building materials were costly in Shakespeare's time. The company soon ran out of funds. The only option left to them was to use materials that they already owned in the form of The Theatre. Today, such a project would be difficult and expensive. It would involve cranes and barges. In Shakespeare's times, it would have almost been a fantasy.

But the company was desperate, and on the night of 28 December 1598, the Lord Chamberlain's Men, with some help from friends and supporters, dismantled The Theatre and hid the materials nearby. When the weather improved, they began to transport the timber across the river, where they built the most famous theatre in history: the Globe.

The Globe opened on 12 June 1599 with a performance of *Julius Caesar*. William Shakespeare must have been inspired by the new venue. His next few plays are among his finest. It is at the Globe that he began to dig deep into his characters and grapple with complex philosophical problems. *Hamlet* followed in the same year, and with the famous 'to be or not to be' line, remains one of Shakespeare's most important works. It explores philosophical questions that continue to challenge audiences. It also contains numerous references to acting, actors and theatres. Shakespeare uses the visit of a travelling theatre company to Hamlet's castle at Elsinore to comment on the state of London theatre. Rival theatre companies are one of his targets.

At the same time that the Globe was being built, a company composed entirely of boys called the Children of the Chapel was attracting large audiences. Shakespeare, a nervous investor in his expensive new theatre, couldn't help launching an attack. Rosencrantz tells an 'astonished' Hamlet about the 'little eyases that cry out on top of the question and are most tyrannically clapped for.' He says that, 'they are now the fashion.' When the actors arrive, Hamlet delivers a speech to them that would appear to contain Shakespeare's views on acting. He advises against grand gestures ('do not saw the air too much') and yelling ('I had as lief [would rather] the towncrier spoke my lines.') Shakespeare's experience as an actor is clear in this remarkable section of the play, and this speech from Hamlet may be the best document that exists of Shakespeare's ideas on the theatre and acting.

Shakespeare's Globe Theatre

In 1997, a recreation of the original Globe Theatre opened in London, about 250 metres from where Shakespeare's theatre stood. The builders worked hard to replicate the original by using similar materials and construction techniques. It is the only building in present-day London with a thatched roof and the first since they were outlawed after the Great Fire in 1666. Every summer, Shakespeare plays are staged at the new Globe, and audiences can experience the plays as they were originally seen in the early 1600s.

Richard Burbage

Richard Burbage was the leading actor in the Lord Chamberlain's Men. He was the first to play many of Shakespeare's most famous roles including Richard III, Hamlet and King Lear. It is possible that his skills as an actor allowed Shakespeare to create the complex characters that define his plays.

The Globe was the most impressive entertainment venue London had ever seen. The circular shape, (actually a polygon), was meant to suggest a Roman amphitheatre but it also resembled the bear pits. In England, the land of Stonehenge, circles have magical properties. Shakespeare's plays began to include more magic around this time.

And it was big. Enormous galleries rose from the ground and historians have estimated that it held more than 3000 people. The stage itself was simple. There was a balcony for Romeo to climb and a trapdoor in the floor where Hamlet could fight with Laertes in Ophelia's grave. The walls were filled with ornate and elaborate engravings painted in garish colours. Everything about the Globe, even its name, suggested a whole world within its circular frame. In *As You Like It,* Shakespeare suggests that 'All the world is a stage'. It is an idea that appears in several of his plays from this period and it would have resonated with the audience who felt themselves transported to other worlds in this magical theatre.

Some historians claim that Shakespeare's original audiences were noisy and poorly behaved during the performances. It is true that a visit to the theatre was a very different experience in 1599, but like today's audiences, people who came were there to see the play.

There were two distinct groups. For two pennies, a seat was available in the one of the galleries. It wasn't particularly comfortable and theft was common. However, the plays were long and a seat made a significant difference, which would explain why the price was double that of the other group.

For a penny a patron could stand on the floor of the theatre. These people were called the 'groundlings'. A somewhat snobby tradition suggests that they were more interested in heckling the actors and socialising than watching the play. It is a even said that they threw food at actors they didn't like, but little evidence exists to support this stereotype. Standing in the 'pit' or 'yard', as the floor was known, would have been uncomfortable and crowded. Restless and tired patrons may have been somewhat unsettled if a play slowed down, particularly after several hours. But the patrons of the Globe were spending hard-earned money to see the plays. For those who wanted something slightly more sophisticated than bears fighting dogs, the theatre was a special experience.

Books were expensive and musical instruments required mastery. Entertainment was a rare commodity and most of the first-hand accounts of visits to the Globe suggest that the audience were there to watch the plays. Some people would show up night after night to watch the same play.

But the audience was not absolutely silent. The good characters were cheered and the bad guys were 'mewed' but there is no evidence that disruptions to the plays were permitted. It is more likely that disruptive groundlings might be dealt some very rough justice and ejected by other members of the audience. The audience members had paid to come in, and they genuinely loved the spectacle.

The spectacle was not restricted to the play it itself. All of Shakespeare's plays involve music and there are more than 300 stage directions that call for musical accompaniment. Shakespeare wrote or adapted more than sixty songs to be sung in the plays. Like movies and television shows today, music was used for atmosphere. Pounding drums built tension and gentle lute music provided the background for romantic moments. The musicians were not hidden in a pit in front of the stage but performed above the balcony facing the audience. The music was one of the main attractions, and it is obvious from the numerous references to music in his plays that Shakespeare knew a fair amount about musical theory.

CHAPTER EIGHT

KNOW YE NOT THAT I AM RICHARD?

Investigator:
Sir Richard Topcliffe
Subject:
Robert Armin

This interview with the informant Robert Armin, a clown and actor with the Lord Chamberlain's Men, was conducted a few days after the Earl of Essex tried to rise up against our glorious Queen. The night before Essex marched into London, he asked the theatre company to put on one of Shakespeare's plays, Richard II. *The play includes a scene where the King is deposed. The Queen was very upset about this, and we are in the process of questioning the actors and members of the company. Clearly the company was paid a large amount of money to stage the play. We are more interested in Shakespeare's connections to Essex, and believe that we have discovered something interesting in this interview — the identity of the notorious Dark Lady!*

Topcliffe: Mr Armin, there are a series of sonnets, I am told, that Will Shakespeare wrote under the patronage of the Earl of Southampton. Do you know the poems to which I refer?

Armin: I have read Mr Shakespeare's sonnets but I must say that I don't much care—

Topcliffe: Yes, yes, I'm sure you have all kinds of clever things to say about them but we want to know only one thing.

Armin: Which is?

Topcliffe: Who is the woman with the violet eyes, the Dark Lady?

Armin: Isn't it obvious?

Topcliffe: Well, not entirely, but we have our suspicions.

Armin: Does he not say something like 'beauty slandered with a bastard's shame'?

Topcliffe: Why yes, he does.

Armin: And doesn't he say, 'Upon that blessed wood whose motion sounds with thy sweet fingers'?

Topcliffe: Yes yes, but what does this all mean?

Armin: I like the bit where he says that 'black wires grow on her head'.

Topcliffe: Mr Armin, please come to the point!

Armin: How many lute-playing dark-hair'd, dark-eyed woman with bastard children can you think of? Who are also known to the Earl of Southampton?

Topcliffe: You don't mean—

Armin: I'm afraid so.

Topcliffe: Lady Penelope Rich! Of course, it all makes sense now.

Armin: Why so?

Topcliffe: How did Mr Shakespeare come to know this woman?

Armin: I don't know. Lady Rich is a clever and talented woman. She plays the lute like an angel and sings heavenly songs. She loves Will's plays and he loves beautiful woman. I think that—

Topcliffe: Yes, but she is the mistress

of Lord Mountjoy and mother of several illegitimate children to him.

Armin: Yes, read the rest of the sonnets. Who do you think his 'sweet'st friend' is? It's Mountjoy! Look, I don't know the details but you'll find the word 'rich' throughout Will's sonnets and plays.

Topcliffe: So, Will Shakespeare was dishonouring not one but two Lords of the realm?

Armin: Well, I don't know about that. Lady Rich's husband, the honourable Lord Rich, surely knows about Mountjoy. I mean, they live together and have five children. It all started when Shakespeare was living on the estate of the Earl of Southampton.

Topcliffe: Southampton, eh, another conspirator…

Armin: Well, yes, but Will was there as a guest during the Plague summer of '93. He wrote the sonnets as an amusement for the Earl. Lady Rich was another visitor to the estate that summer. Will, as you know, is married to a woman in Stratford. She is a kind and gentle type, but Lady Rich was something altogether different.

Topcliffe: What do you mean?

Armin: This woman challenged him on everything. Look at *Romeo and Juliet*. That is Will and Lady Rich. I don't mean that they were teenage lovers, but Juliet is beautiful and clever. Romeo never has a chance. Think about Portia in *The Merchant of Venice*, Katherine in *The Taming of the Shrew*, Rosalind in *As You Like It*. I think they are all Lady Rich.

Topcliffe: Are you aware that Lady Rich has had some contact with Catholic elements? She is the sister of the Earl of Essex — might she have had some involvement with his rebellion?

Armin: No idea. But I can tell you that Shakespeare was never interested in her religion. It was her — her mind, her beauty and her words. He said that she was a new kind of woman and that he wanted to celebrate this in his plays. Will isn't interested in political rebellion or overthrowing monarchs. His game is much bigger. He wants to put something on the stage that no one has ever seen before.

Topcliffe: What?

Armin: People! You, me, Lady Rich! 'All the world's a stage.' That's what Will says. The future isn't Catholics and Protestants—

Topcliffe: Careful, clown.

Armin: The future is people!

We ended the interview here. We learned nothing useful about Shakespeare's connection with Essex, though the clown did confirm that the lady in the poems was Lady Penelope Rich. Armin's comment about the future is interesting, though it is not clear exactly what he means. We shall continue to monitor the playwright carefully.

HOW A PLAY BECAME MUCH MORE THAN A PLAY AND NEARLY FINISHED SHAKESPEARE'S CAREER

In Elizabethan London, clapping too enthusiastically could be very dangerous to one's health. When Robert Devereaux, the Earl of Essex, was charged with high treason, a key piece of evidence was a report that he had greeted a particular scene in a play with 'great applause'.

The play was *Richard II* and the offending scene was of the title character being deposed as King. The writer was William Shakespeare, a cautious man when it came to political matters. It must have been a terrible shock to him when one of his plays was responsible for one of the most dangerous moments in his life.

The stepfather of the Earl of Essex, the Earl of Leicester, had been the Queen's favourite and quite possibly her lover in the early years of her reign. Essex was much younger than Elizabeth, but he was handsome and knew how to flatter the ageing monarch.

He was also impulsive and quick to fight if he thought his honour was at stake. The Queen indulged him to a point but drew the line at appointing his friends to offices and positions in government.

Richard II

In Shakespeare's time, this was his most controversial play. It is the story of the English King, Richard II who was removed from the throne by Henry IV in 1399. The suggestion that a monarch could be replaced was not well regarded by the authorities in Elizabethan England. The actual scene where the King is deposed was not published with the rest of the play, and was rarely performed.

In 1601, on the eve of his unsuccessful rebellion, the Earl of Essex commissioned a performance of the play that included the banned scene. Shakespeare's theatre company came under close scrutiny from the Privy Council for that performance.

In 1598, England suffered a number of defeats in Ireland. While the Irish themselves were not likely to invade England, they remained fiercely Catholic, and the English authorities feared that the Irish might allow their country to become a staging ground for a Spanish invasion. To maintain authority, Elizabeth would need to launch a major offensive against the rebels in Ireland. Her problem was finding the right person to lead the English forces. Potential candidates like Sir Walter Raleigh knew that Ireland was ungovernable, and that the inevitable defeat would be a major misstep for anyone interested in maintaining their position in the English court.

Ireland

The Tudor period in England represents the beginnings of a troubled relationship with Ireland that would continue for centuries. Ireland remained defiantly Catholic through Henry VIII's rule, and is still predominately a Catholic country today. Elizabeth spent millions of pounds attempting to subdue the population, but was defeated over and over. The lack of a central government in Ireland made any kind of rule difficult. England's main concern with Ireland in this period was that it would become a staging ground for the much feared Spanish invasion. The Irish population was hostile to English Protestantism, and therefore believed to be sympathetic to Catholic Spain.

Eventually, the Queen called together her inner circle, including the Earl of Essex, and announced that his uncle, William Knollys, would lead the mission. Essex, in his arrogance, saw this as an attack on his own standing. He was furious and he shouted at the Queen. Then he did something unforgivable. He turned his back on her. This show of disrespect prompted the Queen to step forward and slap Essex on the ears. Taken by surprise, he swung around with his hand on his sword. If he had drawn it, he would have lost his head. As he stormed out, he muttered something about her father Henry VIII being the better monarch. As the Queen's father had beheaded her mother, this was a stinging criticism. The Queen was not amused.

Ironically, to get back into the Queen's good graces, Essex agreed to lead the English army to Ireland himself. It was an insane decision, but typical of the arrogant and not terribly bright Earl. Shakespeare's *Henry V* played to enthusiastic crowds in the lead-up to Essex's departure. The play reminded Londoners of a glorious moment in English history when a handsome young King led his small army to victory over the French at the famous battle of Agincourt. Stirring speeches captured the public mood. The most famous is from King Henry himself:

Once more unto the breach, dear friends, once more;
Or close the wall up with our English dead.
In peace there's nothing so becomes a man
As modest stillness and humility;

But when the blast of war blows in our ears,
Then imitate the action of the tiger;
Stiffen the sinews, summon up the blood,
Disguise fair nature with hard-favour'd rage;

Four hundred years later, these same lines were spoken by Lawrence Olivier in a film version of *Henry V*, inspiring Londoners once again as German bombs fell on their city during the Second World War.

Essex would have attended performances of the original play and must have noted the effect on the audience and the public mood in general. It was a lesson that he filed away for later use.

Lawrence Olivier

Sir Lawrence Olivier was one of the most important actors of the twentieth century. He played many Shakespearean roles on stage and in film. His roles in *Hamlet, Richard III* and *Henry V* brought Shakespeare alive on screen, and made his plays accessible to people who might not otherwise have seen them.

The Irish expedition was a total disaster as everyone had expected. Essex, in a rare moment of good sense, cut his losses and signed a peace treaty with the rebels. Unfortunately, he did this without any authority. To make things worse, he immediately returned to England though he had been told to stay in Ireland. On a sunny September morning in 1599, the Queen awoke in her bedchamber to find Essex shouting at her. It was a bad start to the day; once again, she was not amused. Essex was placed under house arrest and stripped of all of his offices and most of his titles.

He spent two years moping around the house before finally getting angry enough to do something so silly that it would overshadow a life filled with misguided acts. He decided to stage a coup to replace Elizabeth with her distant cousin King James VI of Scotland. It was a bad move because James knew that when Elizabeth died he would inherit the throne anyway, and he had little interest in being part of anything involving Essex. He had the right idea. Unfortunately, not everyone was so lucky.

A few days before the coup, a servant of Essex's made his way over to the Globe Theatre to ask the Lord Chamberlain's Men if they would be interested in staging a play. *Richard II* was the play that Essex requested. Shakespeare should probably have been suspicious. It was one of his early plays and was somewhat controversial. It contained a scene in which the King of England, Richard, was deposed (removed from the throne) by Henry Bolingbroke. Printers in London refused to print the scene and it was rarely performed.

One of the special requests made by Essex's servant was that the scene was included in the performance. The money was good and the Lord Chamberlain's Men agreed.

They performed the play on 7 February. Essex was there, cheering at the deposition scene and watching the reaction of the audience. He must have felt encouraged because the next day he rode into London and announced that he was deposing Queen Elizabeth. No one seemed very interested so he turned around and headed for home. On the way he met a confused group of soldiers who fired a shot that accidentally knocked Essex's hat off. A few weeks later he lost his head as well. The Queen, once again not amused, had finally had enough of the Earl of Essex. If only he had waited. Eighteen months later the Queen died of natural causes and James became King anyway.

Shakespeare and the other members of the Lord Chamberlain's Men were very lucky. Somehow they were able to convince the authorities that they had been innocent of any knowledge of the coup. Their defence was that they had been paid simply to put on a play. The sum was double what they usually received and this is probably what saved them. The truth may have been more complicated. One of Essex's co-conspirators was the Earl of Southampton, Shakespeare's first patron. Essex's sister, Lady Penelope Rich, is a plausible candidate for the Dark Lady role in Shakespeare's sonnets. In any case Elizabeth enjoyed Shakespeare's plays, and the night before Essex's execution, the company was back performing for her at Whitechapel Palace.

It was a rare misstep for Shakespeare. Marlowe's death must have continued to provide ample warning of the dangers for playwrights caught up in politics. Shakespeare had maintained a long and cordial relationship with the Queen for the past fifteen years. In the wake of the *Richard II* controversy she commented, 'Know ye not that I am Richard?', but she nevertheless would have found the playwright a courteous and loyal subject. But as many found out, this wasn't any guarantee that one's head would remain attached to one's body. It is hardly surprising that when James became King, Shakespeare formed a bond with him that left no room for misunderstandings.

The Dark Lady

Many of Shakespeare's sonnets feature a woman called the Dark Lady. The identity of this woman has been the subject of every kind of inquiry, from forensic investigations to an episode of *Doctor Who*. Virtually every notable woman in Shakespeare's time, with the exception of the Queen herself, has come under scrutiny. In all likelihood, she is simply a character created for the amusement of his patron.

Lady Penelope Rich

Penelope Devereaux, later Lady Rich, was the sister of the infamous Earl of Essex, but in her time was famous in her own right. She wrote poetry, played the lute, sang and danced beautifully. It is not known whether she knew Shakespeare, but there has been some speculation that she is the lute-playing Dark Lady in his sonnets.

The Sonnets

Shakespeare also wrote poetry. His most famous poems are 154 sonnets. A sonnet is a poem of fourteen lines with a specific rhyme scheme. Shakespeare's sonnets cover a range of subjects and it appears that they were written for a specific patron. In Shakespeare's time, wealthy patrons would commission poems from writers on particular topics. These poems would be read for entertainment and discussed at social engagements. There is some dispute as to Shakespeare's patron. Some of the poems seem to be urging a young man to marry. The Earl of Southampton, who was Shakespeare's patron for another poem, is one of the main candidates.

CHAPTER NINE

THE CONSCIENCE OF A KING

Investigator:
Sir Robert Cecil,
replacing the late
Sir Richard Topcliffe
Subject:
Robert Armin

Robert Armin has reported to us for his regular interview. As always, he is well spoken and informative. He has helped us with our inquiries into Ben Jonson, but on William Shakespeare he remains somewhat reluctant to share anything of value.
It is possible that there is nothing to share, but Shakespeare is far too an important figure to simply ignore. Though he did not know it, he was a favourite of the late Queen. The new King too seems to find something appealing about this man. We remain curious as to Shakespeare's real motives. Mr Armin, in this excerpt, shares an interesting story about Shakespeare.

Cecil: Mr Armin, the play *Macbeth* was well received by the King and Queen but there is a rumour that it is cursed. Would you tell us more please?

Armin: Please don't say that name again. Yes, the play about the long-ago King of Scotland has been popular, but sometimes I wish he had never written it.

Cecil: Why is that? Surely a man as intelligent as yourself does not believe in curses?

Armin: I wouldn't have six months ago, but that was before Will decided that he needed to include witches in his play. He knew that the King had written a book about witches and that accuracy in this area was critical.

Cecil: What did he do?

Armin: He contacted Dr John Dee, the alchemist or black magician or whatever he is, to ask if he could arrange a meeting with a witch. One afternoon while we were rehearsing at the Globe, a boy appeared with a letter for Will. In the letter was an address in Clerkenwell, a date which was the following day, and a time. It was signed Dr Dee.

Will convinced me to accompany him. We reached the neighbourhood at dusk. Clerkenwell is dangerous enough and I was already on edge at the idea of meeting with witches. We had to pay a local lad to take us to the street. It was a tiny lane and the lad would not take us to the address. In fact, when we got there, he told that us that he would give us our money back if we would just turn around and leave. 'No place for gentlemen,' said the boy. 'We're actors,' said Will. 'If it's a brothel, well the world is one.' The boy turned and ran.

We walked up the winding lane, the only sound being our boots on the cobblestones. The house was the thirteenth on the street, the one with the black door. I was leaning towards the boy's idea of turning around, especially now that night had fallen and the only light was a candle that Will had thought to bring. He knocked at the door. There was no sound but the candle suddenly went out. The door opened but we couldn't see who had opened it.

'Shall we go in?' Will said.

I said, 'No we shall not!'

But he stepped through the door and I reluctantly followed. We found ourselves in a room with a fire. I could make out three figures. They looked like women but it was hard to tell. One had a beard.

'All hail William Shakespeare of the Lord Chamberlain's Men.'

'Yes,' said Will. 'That's me.'

'All hail William Shakespeare of the King's Men.'

'The King's Men?' said Will. 'No, you were right the first time.'

'All hail William Shakespeare. Greatest of all writers.'

Will turned to look at me. It was dark but he seemed to have turned pale.

'What's wrong Will? It all sounds quite good. And what about me?'

'All hail Robert Armin. The fool who isn't.'

'That's all? Not the greatest comic of all time?'

'No.'

'Oh,' said I.

Will had come to ask the women something but he seemed to forget what it was that he wanted to say, and suddenly decided that it was time to leave. The witches cackled away as we left. When we got outside, I asked him what was wrong.

'Nothing,' he said. 'And we might keep this between us, Bob.'

A week later, the Lord Chamberlain's Men became the King's Men. Will refused to meet my gaze when the announcement was made.

A few months later, we began to rehearse *Macbeth*. Will had an idea of the witches scene as a masque and decided that he would have real witches perform in these scenes. Somehow, he convinced the three hags we had met that night to visit the Globe. It was a mad idea. They appeared one night quite late when we had been rehearsing, and some of the actors left in terror. Will had obviously been to see them again as he was quite comfortable with them. We all watched, horrified, as he gave them the scripts and asked them to perform the scene.

'Double double, toil and trouble,
Fire burn and cauldron bubble.'

'I don't like this,' said the oldest witch.'

'What do you mean?' asked Will.

'It's silly.'

'Why?' asked Will.

'Because no witch would ever say anything like this.'

A few of us watching began to laugh until Will shot us a nasty look.

'Look, good woman,' said Will. 'This is a play and—'

'I'm not sayin' it,' said the younger witch.

Will was getting annoyed.

'Well, alright, say whatever you like.'

The witches began to sing in what sounded like a foreign language. They were then shrieking and dancing around the stage. Will was trying to stop them when all of the candles suddenly went out. It was completely dark and I felt a chill at the back of my head. The shrieking stopped and when Will lit another candle, the stage was empty. An old actor fainted and everyone backed away when Will came towards us.

'Alright,' he said. 'A bad idea. Forget all about it.'

The next day while we were rehearsing, a beam fell from the roof and nearly killed Dick Burbage while he was reading his lines. Later in the afternoon, the young boy playing Lady Macbeth tripped and fell off the stage. He needed his leg set and we had to find another actor. Three days after the witches' visit, most of the cast were refusing to enter the Globe. Will was furious but agreed to bring Dr Dee to the theatre to check whether a spell had been cast. The old magician walked around the theatre until he found a small, wizened frog leg that had been jammed in between two floorboards.

'This is your problem right here,' he said. 'They've put a curse on the theatre and probably on the play.'

'Great news,' said Will. 'That's all I need. What should we do?'

'Try to avoid saying the name of the play. You might fool the spirits.'

'And the theatre?'

'It will burn down.'

We ended the interview here as this story seemed ridiculous and was not providing anything for us to use against Master Shakespeare. The playwright sought out Dr Dee and the witches for purely commercial reasons. He is clearly not involved in the black arts.

HOW GUNPOWDER AND WITCHES HELPED SHAKESPEARE TO WRITE A 'SCOTTISH PLAY'

Actors rarely refer to Shakespeare's play *Macbeth* by name. To name it is bad luck and it is known among theatre people as the 'Scottish Play'. There could be any number of reasons why the title of this play causes so much anxiety. The obvious explanation might be the play itself. *Macbeth* is simply creepy. It opens with three witches and finishes with the title character's head being held up to the audience. In between there is an ever-increasing body count that includes women and children, a pesky ghost that spoils a banquet, and the diabolic Lady Macbeth who loses her mind. The light moments are few and the only comic scene involves a hung-over gatekeeper who imagines he is at the gates of hell. In a memorable speech, Macbeth decides that he has killed so many people that he might as well kill some more. No one would mistake this play for one of the comedies. However, it remains one of

Shakespeare's most popular works. It is short, quick paced, and suspenseful in the manner of a classic crime story. Unlike many of his other plays, it has never gone out of style and it is likely that at any given moment, someone somewhere on earth is watching a performance of *Macbeth*.

Sir Robert Cecil

Robert Cecil, later Lord Salisbury, was the Secretary of State under both Queen Elizabeth and James I. He took over the role of Spymaster and operated England's intelligence network after the death of Francis Walsingham.

The Scottish Play was written for the Scottish King James VI not long after he became James I, King of England. Shakespeare got off to a good start with the new King, and the Lord Chamberlain's Men soon found themselves renamed the King's Men. This meant that they were the leading theatre company in the country and that Shakespeare was effectively the King's playwright. After his brush with the authorities in the wake of the Essex rebellion, Will was anxious to avoid controversy. He did, however, continue to write plays that captured the public mood.

Another play that appeared early in James's reign was *Measure For Measure*. The play involves a Duke who takes a holiday in order to better understand the nature of leadership. Many of the important speeches are quite instructive on the subject. The play contains an important message about the need for balance between justice and mercy. Elizabeth was Queen for a long time and most people had never lived under another monarch. Shakespeare's messages in this play echo the sentiments of a somewhat nervous nation. Playgoers would have been comforted to see these ideas expressed in public. Shakespeare knew how powerful his plays could be in informing public opinion. In *Measure for Measure*, the Duke's temporary replacement immediately sets about closings the brothels of Vienna (where the play is set). This is characterised as an act of extremism in the play. Since both brothels and theatres were at the mercy of the authorities, Shakespeare may have been urging the new King to be kind to his principal source of income.

King Lear is another play from this period. It is a complex play in many ways but its main message is that people have to be nice to each other and that rulers have to listen to good advice. Both of these plays would have certainly struck a chord with Londoners adjusting to the idea of a new king.

The play *Macbeth* followed what has become known

as the Gunpowder Plot. In 1605, a man called Robert Catesby and a group of others decided to blow up the English Parliament while the King was opening a session. It was the kind of plot that the Elizabethan intelligence networks had always anticipated. Hundreds, if not thousands of people had been arrested, questioned and sometimes tortured in an attempt to foil such a plot. The simmering anger of English Catholics had never gone away despite the efforts of Elizabeth's agents. Instead, they were driven further underground and forced to become even better organised. The beginning of James's reign had been promising. His wife was Catholic and he was the son of Mary, Queen of Scots, the Catholic claimant to the English throne. James had promised tolerance, but had instead signed a whole new set of laws designed to persecute Catholics and promote Protestantism. The shadowy world of Catholic England began to stir and by 1604, barely a year into James's reign, an act of terrorism was being planned, designed to destabilise the entire nation.

The New King

When Queen Elizabeth I died in 1603, years of uncertainty about who would be the next monarch ended with the coronation of her distant cousin, James, as King. James I of England was also James VI of Scotland, bringing the two nations together. The current Queen of England, Elizabeth II, remains Queen of Scotland.

A man called Guy Fawkes rented a coal cellar underneath the parliament buildings using the name John Johnson. He had been a soldier in Europe and was in charge of preparing explosives. And there were a lot of explosives. Hidden beneath kindling and firewood was 36 barrels or 5500 pounds of gunpowder. Modern experts estimate that the explosion would have destroyed the parliament buildings and every other building within a 500-metre radius. It very nearly succeeded. Guy Fawkes successfully lodged the gunpowder and parliament was set to open on 5 November. The plan was to blow the King and virtually everyone else of any note to smithereens, and then to put the King's nine-year-old daughter Elizabeth on the throne as a 'puppet' monarch. The planning had been thorough, and had been organised by a group used to secrecy and discretion. It should have worked, but it didn't.

A chain is only as strong as its weakest link, and a man called Francis Tresham proved to be just that for the conspirators. About a week before the opening of parliament, he had an attack of conscience that led him to send a letter of warning to his brother-in-law, Lord Monteagle. He had begun to think about the Catholic members of parliament and how they would also be killed when the explosion took place. Francis Tresham was simply not terrorist material. Tresham's letter, which still exists, said:

'They shall receive a terrible blow this parliament and yet they shall not see who hurts them.'

Lord Monteagle went immediately to the King. The plotters were arrested and most of them executed. The night of fireworks that takes place every year in England on 5 November is still known as Guy Fawkes night. Catholic emancipation in England did not occur for another 200 years.

Shakespeare, who must have felt as though he was watching one of his own plots unfold, used his play *Macbeth* to feed the public appetite for stories of coups and dark plots. As Macbeth conspires with his wife to kill the noble King Duncan, theatre patrons must have felt the tension of instability and treason. Nothing was more valued by Londoners in this period than peace. The Gunpowder Plot awakened memories of religious strife and civil war. In Shakespeare's play, Duncan's murder is so unnatural and evil that it affects, among other things, the natural world. The sun doesn't rise, horses go wild and little birds eat big birds. His audience would have savoured all of this, safe in the knowledge that the plot against their own King had been stopped.

But the Gunpowder Plot isn't the only element of *Macbeth* that would have set Londoners thinking about their own time. It was common knowledge that their new King was very interested in subject of witchcraft. Witches were part of the popular imagination and the charge of witchcraft remained a very serious matter. James had personal experience in this area.

His relationship with his mother, Mary, Queen of Scots, was, to say the least, complicated. After she was executed by her cousin Queen Elizabeth, James discovered that there was a plot to unseat him as King of Scotland. The leader of the rebels was his mother's third husband, the Earl of Bothwell. When the plan was uncovered and the Earl arrested, a search of his residences was carried out. At the Earl's house, a wax figure was discovered. Attached to the leg of the figure was a label that read: 'James'. When he was tortured, the Earl admitted that he had purchased the figure from a witch and intended to burn it. James was horrified but also fascinated. A few years later in 1590, as he was about to embark on a visit to Denmark, three women were discovered to have put a 'curse' on his ship. They had attached live cats to the severed arms and legs of corpses and thrown them into the North Sea. This was an attempt to raise a storm and sink James's ship. James managed to survive the sea journey, but the women were still tried and put to death. The persecution of witches continued in Scotland for more than ten years after these incidents. Nearly 500 so-called 'witches' were tried and executed. In 1597, James published a book on the subject called *Daemononlogie*. For the rest of his life, James pursued an interest in witches. The play *Macbeth* pays tribute to this interest and combines it with a story about Scotland, two subjects sure to catch the attention of playgoers in the early years of James's reign. With the backdrop of political instability and regicide (the murder of a king), *Macbeth*'s dark appeal was guaranteed.

John Dee

Dr Dee was a gifted mathematician, astronomer and cartographer. The Queen consulted him regularly, and he was also rumoured to be a magician. In Shakespeare's time, science was closely associated with magic, and Dee's experiments were regarded with suspicion. He was also famous for his extensive library, and it is likely that the character Prospero in *The Tempest* is based on Dee.

EPILOGUE

When Shakespeare died in 1616 at the age of fifty-three, he left his wife only his second-best bed. Scholars have spent nearly 400 years trying to determine why the greatest writer in the English language would put something so petty in his last will and testament. Shakespeare arrived in London sometime in the late 1580s and worked there until returning to Stratford on a more or less permanent basis about twenty years later. His wife by this point had brought up their three children, suffered the death of Hamnet her son, and probably managed her husband's affairs in Stratford. Anne Shakespeare, nee Hathaway, is one of the great wives of history. So why is she only given the second-best bed? And who got the best one?

Shakespeare never really retired from writing, but he did slow down. After 1607, he only wrote a handful of plays, some of which were collaborations. None, with the possible exception of *The Tempest,* have the depth or power of his earlier works. The sobering truth is that even Shakespeare eventually ran out of great ideas. By 1607, he was forty-three years old and a veteran of the London theatre scene. Young writers like Ben Jonson had begun to provide the competition that had last been supplied by Christopher Marlowe fifteen years earlier. Shakespeare collaborated with younger writers on plays like *Pericles* and *Two Noble Kinsman,* but there is a sense of exhaustion to his final efforts, which is probably understandable.

The First Folio

In 1623, two actors, John Heminges and Henry Condell, published the first complete collection of William Shakespeare's plays. Many of his plays had been published in his lifetime but this collection, known as the *First Folio,* represents the single most important source of Shakespeare's work. The texts of the plays are based on scripts, prompt books and Shakespeare's 'foul papers' (drafts and manuscripts). About 1000 copies were printed, and there are 228 known copies still in existence. Copies of the *First Folio* now sell for many millions of dollars.

Theatrical forms had moved on somewhat by 1607. King James's oldest son, Prince Henry, along with his mother, Queen Anne, favoured a form called the 'masque'. A masque involved costumes, dancing and music. They sometimes involved amateur actors or even members of the audience. They were in some ways like a choreographed costume party. There was a simple story that might be told in song or by an actor, followed by a dance. Ben Jonson cemented his place at court by writing many masques according to the instructions of the Queen. He worked with the architect Inigo Jones to create ornate sets for these performances. The form wasn't new and Shakespeare had included masque elements in earlier plays. The ball scene in *Romeo and Juliet,* for example, may have been performed as a masque. The procession of Scottish kings in *Macbeth* also owes something to this tradition. However, Shakespeare did not join Jonson and other writers like Thomas Campion in composing masques for the Queen and Prince Henry. He may not have felt entirely comfortable with the form. *Cymbeline* was written for a court performance in 1609 and contains masque-like scenes. It is an uncertain play that seems like comedy at points and melodrama at others. Keeping up with fashion can be tricky.

But Shakespeare hadn't gone out of fashion. At least not in Africa, where in 1607, *Hamlet* was performed in Sierra Leone. African tribal chiefs, along with sailors, pirates and slaves, listened to Hamlet's famous soliloquy beginning with 'To be or not be', at the edge of a vast geographical unknown and a new age in world history. Shakespeare might not have known about this particular performance but he was aware that England was beginning to see its future in its overseas lands. Sailors on trade missions to Asia, Africa, the Caribbean and North America, brought back stories that ranged from the outrageous to the scientific. The bottom of the globe, where Australia would soon begin to take shape on European maps, was thought to be inhabited by people whose faces were on their chests. The closer one got to England, the less absurd the stories, but there was enormous curiosity about the ever-growing world.

In this period, Shakespeare had begun to spend time at the Mermaid Tavern in Blackfriars. He is remembered debating with Ben Jonson, but it is likely that he also met a man called Dudley Digges who was a member of parliament. Digges was an investor in the lucrative tobacco plantations in the colony of Virginia. He had also funded figures like William Baffin, who gave his name to Baffin Island, and Henry Hudson, who gave his name to Hudsons Bay in the north of what is now Canada. In particular, Digges funded Hudson's final voyage, which ended in mutiny in the bay that would take his name. His crew simply set him adrift in a small boat and he was never heard from again. It isn't hard to imagine Shakespeare mulling over this story after a night at the Mermaid.

Another trip funded by Digges was a trade mission to Bermuda in 1609, led by a ship called the *Sea Adventurer*. A particularly devastating storm destroyed the ship and left the surviving sailors on an empty island. When they were rescued, one sailor, William Strachy, wrote a terrifying account of his experiences on the island that was passed around at the Mermaid. Shakespeare used his story as the basis for the last play that he would write on his own, *The Tempest*.

It gave him a chance to use a character that he had probably been holding onto for some time. Prospero, the scholar and magician, is based on a man called John Dee who Queen Elizabeth regularly consulted on matters medical, astrological and magical. He was equal parts a scientist, an alchemist and a complete charlatan. He lived in London for most of his life and Shakespeare would have certainly known him. Prospero is the Duke of Milan who has been overthrown and sent to live on a remote island. With his magic he rules over Caliban, a monster of sorts, who claims that the island is his own. Shakespeare recognised that the obvious problem in ruling over colonies is that land taken by force is never truly owned. By the Jacobean period, Native Americans, Africans and Asians were an increasingly common sight in London. Shakespeare imagines the relationship between Prospero and Caliban in a way that has ensured the play has remained relevant for the past 400 years.

But Prospero is also Shakespeare, the magician of the theatre, saying farewell to his audience.

> But this rough magic
> I here abjure: and, when I have required
> Some heavenly music — which even now I do —
> To work mine end upon their senses, that
> This airy charm is for, I'll break my staff,
> Bury it certain fathoms in the earth
> And deeper than did ever plummet sound
> I'll drown my book.

So it would be poetic to say that this was simply the end for Shakespeare in London, and he returned to Stratford for his remaining years to play with his grandchildren. Unfortunately, endings in life are rarely so neat and tidy. He co-wrote at least one more play, the rambling *Henry VIII*. In 1613, it was playing at the Globe when one of the cannons used in the show sent a spark into a curtain. The theatre burnt to the ground. Shakespeare must have found it difficult to look at the charred remains of a venue where his most celebrated masterpieces had played. He returned to Stratford more or less permanently after this and died in 1616 on his fifty-third birthday.

And the second-best bed? Shakespeare had acquired a modest fortune by the time he died. He owned properties in London and his family lived in the grandest house in Stratford. His will left most of his holdings to his daughter Susanna. Anne, his wife, is not mentioned much in the will as she was legally entitled to a third of his estate under the widow's law. She was also allowed to remain in her home. The second-best bed might have referred to a family heirloom, or it might have been a coy expression to describe the marriage bed. It might have been a last slight on a wife he had never really known. It might have been an in-joke between the couple. No one will ever know for sure. But then Shakespeare, like his second-best bed, remains something of a mystery.

APPENDIX I: DRAMATIS PERSONAE

Allen, Edward: Elizabethan era actor.

Allen, Giles: Owned the land on which The Theatre stood.

Arden, Mary: Mother of William Shakespeare.

Armin, Robert: Shakespeare's second clown. A more intellectual fool than Kempe, he was the model for roles such as the gravedigger in *Hamlet* and the fool in *King Lear*.

Baffin, William: English explorer. Baffin Island is named after him.

Ball, Cutting: A notorious criminal in Elizabethan London. An associate of Robert Greene.

Ball, Emma: Sister to Cutting Ball. Mistress of Robert Greene.

Bothwell, Earl of: Third husband of Mary, Queen of Scots. Placed a 'curse' on her son, James, later King of England.

Bradley, William: Son of a pub owner in Elizabethan

London. Killed in a duel with Thomas Watson.
Burbage, Richard 'Dick': Lead actor in the Lord Chamberlain's Men. First man to play Hamlet and many other famous Shakespearean roles.
Burleigh, Lord: A favourite of Queen Elizabeth. Involved in intelligence matters.
Campion, Thomas: Composer, poet and playwright. He wrote masques for James I.
Catesby, Robert: Co-conspirator in the Gunpowder Plot.
Cecil, Sir Robert: Succeeded Lord Burleigh.
Chettle, Henry: Publisher in Elizabethan London.
Dee, Dr John: Magician, alchemist, cartographer, philosopher, astronomer, astrologer and mathematician. An adviser to Queen Elizabeth and the model for Prospero in Shakespeare's play *The Tempest*.
Devereaux, Robert, Earl of Essex: Favourite of Queen Elizabeth who eventually fell out with her. Involved in an unsuccessful rebellion against the Queen and executed for his trouble.
Digges, Dudley: Member of parliament under King James I. He invested in plantations in the New World and financed exploration expeditions.
Dudley, Robert, Earl of Leicester: A favourite adviser to Queen Elizabeth.
Fawkes, Guy: AKA John Johnson. Co-conspirator in the Gunpowder Plot.

Greene, Robert: A writer in Shakespeare's time. Well known for his pamphlets on the 'low life' elements of London.

Hathaway, Anne: Wife of William Shakespeare.

Heminges, John and Condell, Henry: The two actors who put together the *First Folio,* the first complete collection of Shakespeare's plays.

Hudson, Henry: English explorer. Hudsons Bay and the Hudson River in New York are named after him.

Hunks, Harry: A bear.

James I (VI of Scotland): Scottish King who became King of England upon the death of his cousin Queen Elizabeth in 1603.

Jones, Inigo: Architect and set designer in the time of King James I.

Jonson, Ben: Playwright, poet and companion/rival of William Shakespeare. Best-known plays include *Volpone* and *The Alchemist.*

Kempe, Will: Shakespeare's first clown. A share holder in the Lord Chamberlain's Men.

Knollys, William, Earl of Banbury: Adviser to Queen Elizabeth. Known as 'Party Beard' for his colourful facial hair.

Kyd, Thomas: Elizabethan playwright best-known for his play *The Spanish Tragedy.*

Marlowe, Christopher: Elizabethan playwright, poet and spy.

Mary, Queen of Scots: Cousin to Queen Elizabeth,

focus of the plot to restore a Catholic monarch to the throne of England. Mother of James I of England.

Nashe, Thomas: Elizabethan writer and member of the University Wits. Co-wrote the controversial play *Isle of Dogs* with Ben Jonson.

Olivier, Lawrence: Considered to be one of the great actors of the twentieth century. Played many Shakespearean roles on stage and in films.

Poley, Robert, Frizer, Ingram, Skeres, Nicholas: Men present at the murder of Christopher Marlowe. All had connections in the intelligence world.

Raleigh, Walter: Writer, soldier, explorer, courtier. An on-again, off-again favourite of Queen Elizabeth. Noted as a 'stupid git' by John Lennon in The Beatles song, *I'm So Tired*.

Rich, Lady Penelope: A colourful personality in Shakespeare's time. She was a musician and dancer who was married to one nobleman and involved in a long-term relationship with another. Sister of Robert Devereaux.

Sackerson: A bear.

Shakespeare, John: Father of William Shakespeare.

Shakespeare, Judith and Hamnet: Twin children of William Shakespeare.

Shakespeare, Susanna: The daughter of William Shakespeare.

Shakespeare, William: A playwright and actor.

Skelton, Thomas: AKA 'Tom Fool'. A well-known though almost certainly psychotic clown, who claimed to be the court jester. Contributed the term 'tomfoolery' to the English language.
Spencer, Gabriel: Actor in Elizabethan London. Killed by Ben Jonson in a duel.
Strachy, William: A sailor who wrote about the terrifying shipwreck adventure that may have inspired *The Tempest*.
Tarleton, Richard: The first great English clown. A member of the Queen's Men theatre company.
Topcliffe, Sir Richard: The Queen's chief Interrogator.
Tresham, Francis: Co-conspirator in the Gunpowder Plot who warned his cousin, Lord Monteagle, to stay away from the opening of parliament.
Watson, Thomas: Poet and associate of Christopher Marlowe.
Walsingham, Sir Francis: The Queen's Spymaster.
Wriothesley, Henry, Earl of Southampton: Sometime patron of William Shakespeare. Involved in the Essex Rebellion.

APPENDIX 2: PLAYS AND POEMS

William Shakespeare's plays are difficult to date precisely, but this is a rough guide to when they were first performed. The poems are even more difficult to date, but these are rough estimates as to when they were written.

Plays and Poems

1589–1592
Henry VI, Part 1
Henry VI, Part 2
Henry VI, Part 3

1592–1595

Richard III

The Comedy of Errors

Titus Andronicus

The Taming of the Shrew

Two Gentlemen of Verona

Love's Labour's Lost

Romeo and Juliet

Sir Thomas More (Shakespeare may be one of the writers. Through handwriting analysis, he has been identified as 'Hand D'.)

Venus and Adonis (Poem)

The Rape of Lucrece (Poem)

The sonnets (Poems)

1595–1598

Richard II

A Midsummer Night's Dream

King John

The Merchant of Venice

Henry IV, Part 1

Henry IV, Part 2

Edward III (This has only recently been considered one of Shakespeare's plays and remains the subject of some controversy.)

1598–1601

Much Ado About Nothing

Henry V

Julius Caesar

As You Like It

Twelfth Night

Hamlet

The Merry Wives of Windsor

The Phoenix and the Turtle (Poem)

1601–1604

Troilus and Cressida

All's Well That Ends Well

Measure for Measure

Othello

A Lover's Complaint (Poem)

1604–1607

King Lear

Macbeth

Antony and Cleopatra

Coriolanus

Timon of Athens (with Thomas Middleton)

1607–1610

Pericles (with George Wilkins)
Cymbeline
The Winter's Tale

1610–1613

The Tempest
Cardenio (with John Fletcher — play lost)
Henry VIII (with John Fletcher)
The Two Noble Kinsmen (with John Fletcher)

There are also a number of other plays and poems that have, at different times, been accepted as Shakespeare's works. There have also been several reasonably successful hoaxes involving 'lost' works. A play called *Edmund Ironside* is one of the most recent contenders. The story of what was and wasn't written by Shakespeare continues to unfold.

APPENDIX 3:
THE AUTHORSHIP CONTROVERSY

It has to be said that the Shakespeare himself is responsible for the 'who wrote Shakespeare's plays' controversy. If he had left just one diary or journal entry, even a letter or two mentioning how happy he was with the success of *Romeo and Juliet* or one of his other plays, the controversy could have been avoided. His first biographer might have made life easier for everyone if he had made the trip to Stratford to talk to Shakespeare's daughter. He didn't bother, but there is actually plenty of evidence that Shakespeare wrote the plays. There are references in the records of the Master of the Revels under James I, and all kinds of documents that link Shakespeare to the plays that we associate with him, but none of this evidence is good enough for a vast number of people who refuse to believe that a glovemaker's son from Stratford could have written such wonderful works.

There have been more than fifty different individuals suggested as the true author of the plays. Just about every notable figure in Elizabethan England from a doctor who once went to Denmark to the Queen herself has come under the scrutiny of those known as the 'anti-Stratfordians'. Three figures are commonly considered the frontrunners. They are:

Christopher Marlowe: Despite the fact that he died just as Shakespeare was beginning to write his best plays, and despite the fact that his own work is quite different, he remains a strong contender. Some members of the Christopher Marlowe Society aggressively assert that his death was faked and he escaped to Italy where he sent his plays back to a lowly actor named William Shakespeare.

Edward de Vere, the Earl of Oxford: This contender was put forward in 1918 by a man named Thomas Looney. Looney's idea was that de Vere was well educated, well travelled, and spoke Italian. Since many of Shakespeare's plays are set in Italy, it was clear that this man must have written them. Unfortunately, de Vere died in 1604, which means he probably didn't write *Macbeth*, which refers directly to the Gunpowder Plot of 1605. He probably didn't write any of the other plays that appear after 1604 either, unless, like Marlowe, he sent them to Shakespeare — in this case, from beyond the grave!

Francis Bacon: This claim is the earliest chapter in the authorship controversy. In the 1830s a woman called Celia Bacon, who later went mad, decided that her namesake, Francis, was the true author of the plays. Bacon was an important figure in Elizabethan England. He was a philosopher, a parliamentarian and an adviser to the Queen. The fact that he did not like plays, and said so often, doesn't seem to worry the 'Baconians' nor does the fact that his well-documented life does not include any association with anyone connected to the theatre. There is no evidence that he *didn't* write them, but that is hardly something to base a theory on. Bacon is responsible in some measure for a type of logical deduction that led to the scientific method. Applied to the idea that he wrote Shakespeare's plays, logic suggests he did not.

Marlowe, de Vere and Bacon all attended university and this is often cited as evidence that they, instead of Shakespeare, wrote the plays. It is ironic that Robert Greene's fury in 1592 at Shakespeare's lack of education and humble beginnings still lingers in discussions of this man.

FURTHER READING

Shakespeare's Life

There are countless biographies of Shakespeare dating back to the 1600s. These are a few that I found useful as well as readable:

Ackroyd, Peter: *Shakespeare: The Biography*, Doubleday, 2005.

Bryson, Bill: *Shakespeare: The World as a Stage*, HarperCollins, 2007.

Burgess, Anthony: *Shakespeare*, Da Capo, 2002. (originally published in 1970)

Greenblatt, Stephen: *A Will in the World*, Norton, 2005.

Greer, Germaine: *Shakespeare's Wife*, Harper, 2008.

Kermode, Frank: *The Age of Shakespeare*, Modern Library, 2005.

Shapiro, James: *A Year in the Life of Shakespeare:1599*, Faber and Faber, 2005.

Wood, Michael: *In Search of Shakespeare*, BBC Books, 2003.

Christopher Marlowe

There are many books on Marlowe but if you are interested in the details surrounding his death, the following book is recommended:

Nicholl, Charles: *The Reckoning: The Murder of Christopher Marlowe*, University of Chicago Press, 1995.

The Elizabethan Theatre

This book sets Shakespeare among the other playwrights of the time, including Ben Jonson:

Stanley Wells: *Shakespeare and Co.*, Pantheon, 2007.

Websites

There is no shortage of websites dedicated to Shakespeare including the following:

www.shakespeare-online.com — The texts of all of his plays and poems along with all kinds of other information and links to other sites.

www.bardweb.net — More of the same with some interesting items, such as Shakespeare's will.

www.william-shakespeare.info — An informative website with many interesting articles.

www.marlowe-society.org — Join up, if you dare!

www.rsc.org.uk — The Royal Shakespeare Company, with information on Shakespeare's London.

www.rosetheatre.org.uk — The historic Rose Theatre, London.

ABOUT THE AUTHOR

Tony Thompson is a Melbourne-based writer and teacher. He writes for *The Age* and *The Australian* and has taught English in several Melbourne high schools. He is originally from Toronto, Canada, but has lived in Australia for more than fifteen years. After finishing his undergraduate degree at Trent University in Peterborough, Ontario, he left for a short backpacking tour of Ireland. This trip led to years of aimless but interesting rambles in Europe, North America and Asia. In 1992 he took a job teaching English conversation in Tokyo. An evening of karaoke led to a long-term relationship and marriage to an Australian who was also teaching English in Japan. In 1994, he and his wife moved to a small flat in Carlton, which seemed quite large after living in Tokyo. He began his teaching career at Ivanhoe Grammar's Plenty Campus where he taught for four years before moving to Princes Hill Secondary College. In 2002 he relocated to Borneo where, amid the monkeys, feral dogs and students who doubled as smugglers, he taught English. For the first and final time, he also taught Beginner Guitar. Wearying of the long boat-ride to work, he returned to Australia where he continues to teach and write. He lives in the Western Suburbs with his wife and son.

Acknowledgements

I have to thank the students of Princes Hill Secondary College. Their enthusiasm for Shakespeare defies the prevailing wisdom that time could be better spent analysing video games and TV shows. I often run into current and past students at the theatre when a Shakespeare play is being staged. There is no higher reward for an English teacher.

I must also thank my partner Joanne for her patience and support, and our four-year-old son Henry, who often confuses Shakespeare with Bob Dylan, but does have an imaginary dog called Hamlet.

A note from the author

Bear baiting was a cruel spectacle. The bears were mutilated by the dogs and experienced unimaginable levels of pain and suffering. Sadly, bear bating continues in some parts of the world today. The World Society for the Protection of Animals is actively involved in trying to stop the practice and rescue the bears involved. For more information, check the WSPA website:
www.wspa.org.au/campaigns/bearbaiting

TEACHER'S NOTES

Readership: upper primary to middle secondary.

Contents

1 About the book
2 Chapter Summaries
3 Learning activities

1. About the Book

William Shakespeare is the most famous writer in history. His best-known plays include *Romeo and Juliet, Hamlet, Macbeth, Julius Caesar* and *King Lear*. Shakespeare's plays have been performed all over the world in many languages. At any given moment it is likely that, somewhere on earth, a Shakespeare play is being performed.

But who was this man? He was born in 1563 and died in 1616. Other than his plays, he is survived only by his signature on some legal documents. There are no diaries, letters or detailed memoirs by those that knew him. This hasn't stopped hundreds, perhaps thousands, of people from writing biographies of Shakespeare.

This book is divided into fiction and non-fiction sections. The non-fiction combines what is known about the period with what is known about Shakespeare. The fiction sections use similar material along with stories suggested by his plays, and take the form of a series of interviews between the Queen's chief Interrogator and various individuals who knew Shakespeare.

The book focuses on the period from the late 1580s when Shakespeare moved to London, until the time he moved back to Stratford sometime around 1611 or 1612. London was a vibrant city in Shakespeare's time. England was beginning to build the empire that would make it the most powerful nation on earth in the nineteenth century. It was also a city of intrigue and crime. Shakespeare could not have helped to be affected by the bustling atmosphere of the neighbourhoods where he lived while he wrote his plays.

There are many characters in this book and some vocabulary that may be unfamiliar. Therefore the book includes a cast of characters, biographies and explanations of historical events and concepts.

2. Chapter Summaries

Chapter 1: The Cony-Catcher

Shakespeare's London was a rough and ready place. The entertainment was brutal and sport was dangerous. Most of the citizens were drunk. It is no wonder that Shakespeare's plays are so violent.

Chapter 2: Violent Delights

William Shakespeare came from the town of Stratford. His father was a glovemaker and local politician. His mother was a literate woman from an old family in the area. Shakespeare probably attended the local grammar school. When he was eighteen, he married Anne Hathaway. This chapter looks at his life before he arrived in London and the mysterious 'lost years'.

Chapter 3: The Upstart Crow

Shakespeare reappears in history in 1592 when he was attacked in print by another writer named Robert Greene. Greene was a member of a group of writers known as the University Wits. This group included Christopher Marlowe, the playwright Shakespeare would soon rival. Greene's attack was based on the fact that Shakespeare had not attended university.

Chapter 4: A Great Reckoning in a Small Room

In 1594, Christopher Marlowe was killed in pub in Deptford. He had been drinking all day with three companions and apparently became involved in an argument over the bill. That was the official story. The truth is less clear. Marlowe had worked as a spy and his companions all had connections with the intelligence community. The death of Shakespeare's nearest rival remains a tantalising mystery for historians.

Chapter 5: Sorrows in Battalions

In 1596, Shakespeare's only son, Hamnet, died in Stratford. How this affected the playwright is not known but it is not hard to imagine. At the same time, his friend and fellow playwright Ben Jonson ended up in prison after writing a play that made fun of the Queen. He had only been out a year when he was involved in a fight that ended with the death of an actor named Gabriel Spencer. It seemed that Ben Jonson would lose his head but his knowledge of Latin saved his life.

Chapter 6: The Nine Day Wonder

In 1599, Shakespeare's clown, William Kempe, quit the theatre company and danced across England. Shakespeare's plays began to change with the arrival of Robert Armin, Kempe's replacement. The importance of clowns in Shakespeare's work cannot be underestimated.

Chapter 7: The Distracted Globe

Early in 1599, Shakespeare's theatre company, the Lord Chamberlain's Men, was forced to find a new theatre. The lease on the venue known as The Theatre, where many of Shakespeare's early plays were performed, was not renewed. They found a spot on the other side of the river but had no money or materials for a new theatre. The solution was to transport The Theatre across the river. A complicated procedure today, it would have been nearly impossible in 1599. Somehow it worked and the Globe Theatre opened later that year.

Chapter 8: Know Ye not that I am Richard?

In 1601, the Lord Chamberlain's Men were drawn into the ill-fated Essex rebellion. They were paid to play an early Shakespeare play, *Richard II* on the night before the rebellion was to take place. The play is about a king who is deposed by a rival. Shakespeare and his colleagues did not lose their heads but the Queen was not amused.

Chapter 9: The Conscience of a King

When James VI of Scotland became James I of England, Shakespeare's theatre company became the King's Men. Shakespeare wrote the 'Scottish Play', *Macbeth,* for the new King. James was fascinated and somewhat frightened by witches, so Shakespeare included his famous three witches in the play. This was also the period of the Gunpowder Plot which is referenced in *Macbeth* several times.

Epilogue

Shakespeare's last years in London saw him collaborating with other writers, and writing his final masterpiece, *The Tempest*. His Globe Theatre burned down in 1613 and he seems to have more or less retired afterwards. When he died, he left his second-best bed to his wife and enough mysteries to keep scholars guessing for the next 400 years.

3. Learning Activities

Introducing the book

Aim: To introduce and create interest in the book.
Materials: text
Chapter: Introduction

1. Pre-text task: Brainstorming session.
   In small groups the students write down everything they know about Shakespeare — names of plays, famous lines, etc.
   Put responses on the board. Ask why someone who lived so long ago is still so famous.

2. Examination of the book cover.
   What is the title and subtitle?
   Who is the author?
   What does the cover art suggest about the book?

3. Have class read the blurb on back cover.
   What approach has the writer taken with Shakespeare?
   What kind of story will this be?
   What questions does the blurb raise?

4. The Introduction.
   Read the Introduction.
   Why does the writer like Shakespeare?
   What does he mean when he says that the plays 'remind us what odd creatures we are'?
   Think of a writer that you enjoy and write a similar introduction.

Elizabethan London
Aim: To familiarise students with the historical context of the book.
Materials: library, Internet, text
Chapter: 1 and 2

In small groups research the following topics and report back to the class.

1. Queen Elizabeth I
2. The City of London 1550–1625
3. Religion in Elizabethan England
4. Entertainment in Elizabethan London
5. Sports in Elizabethan London

History as a Story

Aim: To consider the process of writing history.
Materials: text

In groups, answer the following questions:

1. Where do historians find information? Think of as many sources as possible.
2. What do historians do when they find a gap in a story, or when they cannot find sources for a particular event? Think of several possibilities.
3. Is it okay for historians to make up stories? Why or why not?

All biographers of Shakespeare are forced to deal with a period called the 'lost years'. In 1585, Shakespeare signed the baptism certificate of his twins. In 1592, he reappeared when a writer called Robert Greene called him an 'upstart crow' and warned other writers to watch out for this new playwright. There is no record of what Shakespeare did during the seven years in between. What historians and biographers know is that in 1585, Shakespeare was a young father living in Stratford. When he reappears, he is a playwright on the rise in London.

Activity:
What did Shakespeare do during the 'lost years'? You are the historian. Come up with a theory. Think about what you know about his life as a playwright. Are there any clues in his plays? A theory must be supported with facts. Write up your ideas and present them to the class. Put the various theories on a chart. Which one is most credible? What is Tony Thompson's theory? Do you agree?

Christopher Marlowe

Aim: To familiarise students with one of Shakespeare's contemporaries
Materials: library, Internet, text
Chapter: 3

1. Research Christopher Marlowe and write a short profile. Remember that a profile has to focus on what is important. There are plenty of facts about

Marlowe. What is important? The names of his plays and poems? His university career? His childhood? His activities as a spy? His death?

2. There is no evidence as to the nature of the relationship between Shakespeare and Marlowe. There are references to Marlowe's death in *As You Like It* and possibly in the sonnets. Tony Thompson believes that Shakespeare was profoundly affected by Marlowe's death. What effect does he believe that Marlowe's murder in 1593 had on Shakespeare?

3. Write a letter from Shakespeare to his wife, Anne Hathaway, in Stratford, dated 1593. Include Marlowe's death and his feelings about this event along with any other information that you think she might find interesting.

Ben Jonson

Aim: To put the events surrounding Ben Jonson's arrest and subsequent release in a modern context
Materials: text
Chapter: 5

Group activity:

You are the team responsible for putting together a story on a popular current affairs program on London TV, 1598. Ben Jonson has just been released from prison. Everyone is talking about him and the producer of the show wants a story now!

Steps:

1. Brainstorm some possible sequences that you could have in the report. Think about what you see in contemporary current affairs reports — interviews, background information, etc.
2. Write a script and decide who will play the various roles.
3. Perform the report for the rest of the class.

Clowns

Aim: To learn about the history and tradition of clowns

Materials: library, Internet, text

Chapter: 6

Choose one of the following to research and present to the class:

- Clowns in the Middle Ages

- Clowning traditions — choose one tradition to focus on
- Shakespeare's clowns
- Court jesters
- A famous clown (pre-1950)
- A famous contemporary clown
- Clowns and circuses
- Clowns and the cinema

The Globe Theatre

Aim: To consider the Globe Theatre as a commercial venture in the contemporary sense.
Materials: poster paper, markers, text
Chapter: 7

Group Activity:
You work for an advertising agency and have just been given the Globe Theatre account. The owners, Richard Burbage and William Shakespeare, are very keen that the theatre gets off to a good start. They have taken a big risk and gone into debt to get their theatre up and running. The advertising campaign must be good! They will need:

- A slogan or a catchy phrase that defines the theatre
- A logo

- Theme music (from any era)
- A TV ad campaign

Before you begin to design these items, you will need to discuss the following:

- The 'brand' — what kind of a place is the Globe Theatre?
- The audience — who is going to attend the Globe Theatre?

The campaign can be offbeat, traditional, wild or sombre. You must decide what will work best.

The Dark Lady

Aim: To introduce a famous historical mystery
Materials: the sonnets, library, Internet, text
Chapter: 8

1. Read Shakespeare's sonnets 127 and 128. Discuss the woman described. What does Shakespeare say about her? What can we guess? Why are historians and biographers so fascinated by this person?
2. Using the Internet, find at least three theories on her identity. Present your findings to the class.
3. Read the fiction section of Chapter 8 in the book.

Who is Tony Thompson's candidate? How does he support his claim?

Activity:
You are a gossip columnist in the 1590s. Write a short piece on Shakespeare's Dark Lady using the style of gossip columnists.

The Witches

Aim: To introduce *Macbeth* and the witches
Materials: *Macbeth* — Act One, Scene 1, Act Four, Scene 1 Lines 1-43, library, Internet, text
Chapter: 9

1. In small groups, read the witches scene aloud. Decide how you want to present it and rehearse it. Present it to the class.
2. As a class, discuss the enduring appeal of witches. Why are people so interested in witches?
3. Read Chapter Nine and choose one of the following topics to research. Present your findings to the class:

- Witchcraft in Elizabethan and Jacobean England
- Doctor John Dee
- King James I and witchcraft
- The curse of *Macbeth*

Shakespeare's Plays

Aim: To become familiar with the titles of Shakespeare's plays

Materials: pens, paper, text

Chapter: Appendix

Activity:

Choose a title of one of Shakespeare's plays. This will be the title of a short story you are going to write. You can use ideas from the play or you can make up something completely new. When you submit or read your story aloud, include a few sentences about how you were inspired by the title of the play.

INDEX